MW00811815

Praise for the Raine Stockton Dog Mystery Series

"An exciting, original and suspense-laden whodunit... A simply fabulous mystery starring a likeable, dedicated heroine..."
--*Midwest Book Review*

"A delightful protagonist...a well-crafted mystery."
--*Romantic Times*

"There can't be too many golden retrievers in mystery fiction for my taste."
--*Deadly Pleasures*

" An intriguing heroine, a twisty tale, a riveting finale, and a golden retriever to die for. [This book] will delight mystery fans and enchant dog lovers."
---*Carolyn Hart*

"Has everything--wonderful characters, surprising twists, great dialogue. Donna Ball knows dogs, knows the Smoky Mountains, and knows how to write a page turner. I loved it."
--*Beverly Connor*

"Very entertaining… combines a likeable heroine and a fascinating mystery… a story of suspense with humor and tenderness."

--*Carlene Thompson*

HIGH IN TRIAL

A Raine Stockton Dog Mystery Book #7

By Donna Ball

www.donnaball.net
Published by Blue Merle Publishing
Drawer H
Mountain City, Georgia 30562
www.bluemerlepublishing.com
ISBN 13:978-0-9857748-1-3
ISBN-10: 0985774819
First printing March 2013

Experts in the North Carolina criminal justice system and in the rules and regulations of AKC agility will please forgive certain liberties taken by the author for the sake of this story. No claims made herein should in any way be construed to be an accurate representation of either organization.

Many thanks to Brinkley, Gunny, and Bryte for the use of their names and breeds, although all other details relating to them are entirely the product of the author's imagination. The owners/handlers depicted in this novel are wholly fictitious and bear no known resemblance whatsoever to their real-life counterparts.

This is a work of fiction. All places, characters, events and organizations mentioned in this book are either the product of the author's imagination, or used fictitiously.

Cover by Sapphire Designs
http://designs.sapphiredreams.org/

CHAPTER ONE

December 1992

The rust-colored pickup truck came out of nowhere, careening into the intersection like a skier taking off on a slalom course. There was no way she could have avoided it, even if the road had not been icy, even if the night had not been pitch black, even if she had not had a glass of wine—or maybe two—at dinner. She didn't have time to cry out, and before her foot could even hit the brake, her Taurus had gone into a spin. Headlights flashed in her eyes, the steering wheel wrenched itself from her hand, and her companion shouted, "Steer into the skid! Steer into it!"

She grabbed the wheel, twisted it hard to the right, fought the foot that wanted to slam into the brake pedal. She remembered—she would never forget—the instant her headlights caught the face of the driver of the other vehicle and seemed to freeze it in time: small, terrified eyes, white skin, scruffy beard, and stringy brown hair. His mouth formed an obscenity, revealing one tooth missing in front, before the night snatched him away and she heard the piercing shriek of metal on metal, smelled the burn of rubber, and the car shuddered to a stop. The pickup truck careened off her front bumper, spun around, and screeched to a stop facing north in the southbound lane ten feet away.

For the longest time, she could hear nothing but the sound of her own thundering heartbeat, the hic and gasp of her breath, and, oddly, the hiss of the car's heater, still blowing hot air across the interior. Then she became aware of the man in the seat beside her, dragging off her seat belt, touching her arms and her face, saying, "Sweetheart, are you all right? Talk to me. Are you hurt?"

"Fine, I'm fine. The other fellow… Do you have your phone? Call 9-1-1."

She fumbled for the door handle, but he stopped her with a hand firmly on her wrist.

"Wait," he said. He had an authority about him that could command armies: quiet, calm, calculated, and always in control. It was this she had first loved about him. He didn't panic. He didn't rush to judgment. And he didn't make mistakes. "You've been drinking. I'll go check on him. Change seats with me."

She stared at him. Her voice, normally so gentle, her tone so dulcet, deteriorated into a near hiss of horror. "Me? You've had more to drink than I have! What if he recognizes you? You're supposed to be in Seattle! Think this through, ~~for God's sake—~~"

"I have." His hand was already on the passenger doorknob, and with the other hand he thrust his phone at her. "Call it in. He could be hurt."

He had one foot out the door when the blare of a horn tore through the night. The engine of the pickup truck revved and its driver rolled down his window. "██████!" he screamed out the window. "~~Crazy ████ ████~~! Keep it on the damn road, will you? ~~Crazy ████~~!"

And then, incredibly, the transmission shrieked into reverse, he turned the truck around, and the tires squealed as he sped away.

3

That turned out to be the biggest mistake of that young man's life. And, for the two people watching incredulously as he peeled off, perhaps the luckiest break of theirs. For a time, anyway.

Two hours later, a bored and sleepy patrolman outside a small North Georgia town pulled over a rust-colored pickup truck for speeding and failure to maintain a lane, ran the plates and discovered two DUIs and an outstanding bench warrant. This, and the suspect's erratic behavior, gave him cause to search the vehicle, where he discovered a small cellophane bag containing a trace amount of a white powdery substance that might have been cocaine, a thirty-eight special concealed in the glove box, along with a wad of cash that amounted to two thousand fourteen dollars and a crumpled receipt for gas from a mini-mart outside Hansonville, North Carolina. The officer also noted minor damage to the front right fender of the vehicle that appeared to be recent. The suspect, one Jeremiah Allen Berman, was cuffed and booked on DUI, possession of a concealed weapon, and suspicion of trafficking controlled substances.

At eight o'clock that morning those charges were dropped in favor of far more interesting ones. Apparently a man matching Berman's description, driving a brown or red pickup truck, had stopped for gas at the Cash-N-Carry outside Hansonville, North Carolina, robbed the cash register of over two thousand dollars, and shot the clerk with a thirty-eight caliber weapon before departing, scraping his right front fender on the concrete pylon beside the pump as he fled. Jeremiah Allen Berman was extradited to North Carolina on armed robbery charges, protesting his innocence and demanding his rights every mile along the way.

He was arraigned within forty-eight hours and a trial date was set. The prosecutor offered three years and his court-appointed attorney told him to take it. At first he was cocky. Why were they cutting him a deal if they were so sure he was guilty? Because they couldn't prove it, that was why. Because they didn't have a security camera tape or a bullet or anything but a couple of half-witted witnesses to put him at the scene. Plus, he was innocent. He was totally going to skate if it went to a jury. Meanwhile, the Hanover County jail was clean and the food wasn't half bad. He'd take his chances.

By the time he started to reconsider his decision a few days later, it was too late. The store clerk was dead, and Jeremiah Allen Berman was facing the death penalty for a murder he did not commit.

THE PRESENT

FRIDAY

Donna Ball

CHAPTER TWO

Twenty-nine hours before the shooting

I've always thought I'd like to write a book entitled *Everything My Dog Needs to Know My Mother Taught Me*. My mother wasn't a dog trainer. But she was a great mother. Aside from how to tie my shoelaces and the importance of regular dental checkups, she imparted quite a few important life lessons, such as:

—Honesty is the best policy. It's easier than lying and usually has fewer consequences.

—Always do your best. Less is cheating.

—Winning is better than losing. Always.

Okay, so the meaning of that last one is probably more like *trying* to win is its own reward, or perhaps even it's not whether you win or lose, but how you play the game. I have to admit, I've always been a little on the competitive side. A teacher once described me, somewhat generously, as goal-oriented. My goal is winning.

My name is Raine Stockton. My father was a judge and my mother was the arbiter of all things gentle and proper in the small Smoky Mountain town of Hansonville, North Carolina, where I still live. I'm afraid I've fallen a little short of her standards when it comes to gentility and propriety, but I do try my best to impart to my dogs the same important life lessons she taught me. Honesty, for example, is as desirable a quality in a dog as it is in a human, and you hear a lot of talk about "honest" dogs on the competitive circuit. Frankly, I've never met a dishonest dog, but when trainers and handlers call a dog honest, what they usually mean is he's consistent, dependable, and earnest. What you see is what you get.

My golden retriever Cisco is extremely consistent: consistently distractible, consistently curious, consistently unpredictable. For example, with only one group ahead of us for our very first run of the agility season—the one that would set the tone for the rest of the year—he was completely and obsessively focused, not on me, his partner, his handler, and the only member of our two-member team who could actually read the course map the judge designed, but on Brinkley, a sassy golden retriever who'd recently become his new BFF.

Brinkley, good dog that he was, was warming up by weaving through his handler's legs and practicing focus by dropping to a sit on command and maintaining eye contact. Cisco watched him in eager fascination, ears forward and grinning, as I sank down onto the bleachers, tugging him into place beside me. The Excellent class was finishing up; Open—in which we were entered—was next. Cisco had completed walk time, play time, warm-up time at the practice jump, and a pep talk. I was wearing my lucky Golden Retriever Club of America sweatshirt, my lucky agility socks, and the Air Bud cap my young friend Melanie brought back from her spring break trip to Disney World in Orlando. My shoelaces were double knotted. My long brown ponytail was threaded through the back of my hat, securely out of my way. I was ready. Cisco was ready. There was nothing more we could do until the judge called our class.

We'd traveled from Hansonville to Pembroke, South Carolina, for the three-day AKC sanctioned agility trial, which was the traditional opening of the competitive season in our part of the country. It was a gorgeous April weekend, and the venue was perfect: huge open agricultural fairgrounds and exhibition center with two covered pavilions, a concrete livestock building for crating, plenty of public restrooms, a separate concessions building surrounded by picnic tables, and acres of rolling grass for setting up shade canopies and walking dogs. There was even RV parking on site, and every time I walked past the camping area with the smell of charcoal-grilled burgers and the sight of happy dogs lounging in their ex-pens in front, I felt a stab of yearning. Although I had no complaints about my luxurious room at the Pembroke Host Inn on this trip, most doggie motels left a great deal to be desired. An RV was any dog show enthusiast's secret dream.

If I had had an RV, for example, I would have brought my two Aussies, Mischief and Magic, and I would have entered every class being offered this weekend. I might even have a chance of winning one. On the other hand, Cisco and I had trained all winter—well, part of it, anyway—and I was feeling good about our chances. I only hoped Cisco shared my confidence.

Of course, there were a few advantages to

staying in a motel rather than an RV, even if it did mean limiting myself to one dog. Like room service, for example, and a full stand-up shower. And the fact that my boyfriend, Miles, had surprised me by driving in from Atlanta last night and had immediately upgraded our room to a mini-suite. I have to admit, the evening wouldn't have been nearly as enjoyable had we been staying in an RV with three dogs.

I always feel a little silly saying that—"boyfriend"—partly because I don't think any woman over sixteen should call any man a boyfriend and partly because, well, I don't exactly know what else to call him. For one thing, Miles is hardly a boy. He's in his mid-forties with short spiky salt-and-pepper hair, a rock-hard body, and nice gray eyes. He has questionable political opinions, a bullheaded way of getting what he wants, and more money than I even want to know about. He's funny and charming and smart, and he makes me laugh even when I'm mad at him. When we're together, he always cooks. He's also the dad of one of my favorite people in the world, the aforementioned ten-year-old Melanie, who'd begged to forgo a school field trip to Washington, D.C., this weekend in order to attend this trial.

Melanie had aspirations of seeing her own golden retriever puppy, Pepper—who was currently in the very capable care of their housekeeper in Atlanta— bring home a slew of blue ribbons one day. While I agreed with her father that a hands-on experience in American government should take priority for the weekend, I also secretly agreed with Melanie that it's never too soon to start exposing a puppy to competition.

The upside of having Melanie in Washington was that Miles and I had the weekend to ourselves—if you didn't count the three hundred or so dogs between us—which was something we'd learned to value since our relationship had taken a more romantic turn. Is he my boyfriend? I still struggle with that. But what else do you call someone who drives four hours just to watch you compete in an event that lasts less than a minute?

Here's something else my mother taught me: Be careful who you date, because you can't always choose who you fall in love with.

"So," said Miles, snapping open a bag of corn chips, "explain the rules to me again."

An agility trial is always more fun with a buddy—someone to cheer you on, help with strategy, and keep you from going bonkers between runs. Usually I trial with Maude, my business partner, oldest friend, and the best dog trainer I know, but since we were rather desperately trying to keep Dog Daze, our boarding and training center, above water we agreed the business could spare only one of us per weekend. This was my weekend, and while it's true that trialing with Maude was both educational and supportive, Miles was a lot more fun. For one thing, I liked seeing the game through the eyes of someone who was new to it, and what girl doesn't like that slightly superior feeling that comes along with explaining things to her guy? For another thing, I'd recently discovered he was almost as much of a junk food junkie as I was, and as everyone knows, dog shows are junk food nirvana.

He offered me the bag of chips, but I shook my head—bad idea to load up on corn chips before a run—and explained, "Okay, right now we're watching the Excellent B Class, which is pretty much as hard as it gets. What's more, this is the twenty-inch jump height group—border collies and Aussies, mostly, who are some of the fastest dogs in the world. Unless you actually *have* a border collie or an Aussie, you really don't want to be in that group. Those numbers on the cones beside each piece of equipment mark the course. The object is to get your dog to follow the numbers faster and with fewer mistakes than any other dog. The trick is that you have to memorize the course and you don't get to practice it with your dog beforehand. But you see the way they're arranged in loops and figure eights and weird triangles? The handler has to do some pretty fancy maneuvering to get his dog from one obstacle to the other without tripping over him. You're not allowed to touch your dog. You get disqualified if you do. It's all done with body language and voice commands. The team with the fastest time and the fewest faults wins first place, and at the end of the weekend, the dog with the highest overall score wins high in trial."

There was, of course, a great deal more to it than that, but most people who weren't themselves agility competitors would have a hard enough time following the action even with that broad outline of the rules. Miles, however, was unfazed. In the short time I'd known him I discovered his interests were eclectic and his curiosity unbounded; he had very little trouble catching on to new things.

"Hmm." Miles watched a border collie sail off the teeter-totter and dash through the tunnel. The judge's hand flew up. "So, do people bet on these things or what?'

"What do you mean, bet?"

"You know, like at the dog track. The greyhounds." He dug into the bag again, focused on the Australian shepherd who was sailing over the first set of serpentine jumps. Cisco turned to him hopefully, the crinkling of the bag having successfully drawn his attention away from Brinkley.

"Of course not." I was mildly offended. "Don't be silly."

"Then what's the percentage?" He started to sneak a corn chip to Cisco, caught my look, and pretended innocence as he popped the chip into his own mouth instead. "Who pays for the training, the prizes, the shows? What do you get out of it?"

"Entry fees pay for the shows," I explained patiently, "and the sponsoring dog clubs do all the work. As for the prizes—a few hundred dollars cover the ribbons and dog toys. What did you think, there was a jackpot cash prize for high in trial?" I shrugged. "We do it for the fun of it, that's all. It's a game."

He gave a slow shake of his head. "Wasted opportunity," he said. "If Vegas ever gets word of this, look out."

I helped myself to a chip—okay, a couple of chips—and gave him a suspicious look. "Okay, you don't drink, you don't smoke, you hardly ever swear, and you don't mind driving four hours to watch a dog show. So gambling's your vice, right? You've got bookies lined up from here to Atlantic City and you drop a couple grand every weekend on football."

"I work too hard for my money to gamble with it," he replied mildly. "Whoa, look at that little guy go. Are you watching that, Cisco? That's the time to beat."

Cisco grinned at him happily, ears pricking with renewed expectation as he watched Miles's hand dive into the bag again.

"Whatever you do," I told him sternly, "don't feed my dog."

"Wouldn't dream of it."

"And make sure that bag is out of sight before we go into the ring."

"You got it."

"There are AKC regulations about training on the grounds, you know. And food in the vicinity of the ring is absolutely forbidden."

"Easy, sweetheart. Like you said, it's just a

game."

I gave him a look known to send large dogs trembling to their crates. I could see him fight back a grin as he crumpled up the empty bag and took out his phone. "Don't worry," he said, scrolling through his messages. "No food, no training, no ~~pissing~~ off the judge. Horse racing is just a game, too, you know, but two people have been murdered at the Kentucky Derby in the past ten years alone over a horse."

I stared at him. "How do you *know* things like that?"

He shrugged, not looking up from his phone. "I keep up."

I rolled my eyes elaborately, and a woman taking a seat a few feet away from me caught the expression and grinned. "Husbands," she said.

"He's not my husband," I objected quickly.

Miles said at the same time, "Not her husband."

That caused me to frown at him a little. I couldn't say why, but he was still checking messages and didn't notice. The woman, who should by now have no doubt as to the nature of our relationship, nodded at Cisco. "Great dog," she said. "I was watching you warm up. He's got real heart."

I rubbed Cisco's ears and said proudly, "Thanks." Cisco, who always knew when he was being complimented, tilted his head back to grin at me. "This is Cisco, and I'm—"

"Raine Stockton," she said. "I know."

Cisco and I are pretty well known in our hometown, both for our search-and-rescue work and as a therapy dog team. We get our pictures in the paper now and then, and if there's a fundraiser for the humane society, I'm always the one who does the radio interview. But had our fame spread as far as Pembroke, South Carolina? Even my ego was having trouble believing that.

My surprise must have been evident because she explained. "I recognized you from your Facebook page."

"Oh." I relaxed. Everyone in dogs was on Facebook and Twitter; we posted action shots of our champions to each other's timelines and tweeted our triumphs like gleeful children. I tried to remember if I'd seen this woman's picture anywhere before.

"I'm Aggie Connor," she went on, reaching across the bleacher to extend her hand. "Celestial Goldens."

Of course she was. The sweatshirt she wore had

the kennel name, Celestial Goldens, written in script above the happy face of a golden retriever on the front. Since the AKC frowned upon apparel that identified a dog to the judge, I assumed she must be here to watch someone else complete. She was a large woman in her forties or fifties with short curly hair and work-worn hands, and as I shook one of those hands, I made the connection.

"I know who you are," I said, relieved to be out of the dark. "My friend, Maude, has Sundance Goldens." The dog show world is a relatively small one, and the chances are good that you will meet someone you know, or almost know, at every show.

She grinned. "I know. My daughter Ginny is running Gunny in Novice. One of Maude's dogs is Gunny's sire."

I nodded. "Sure, I know Ginny and Gunny." In fact, I'd never met Ginny, but had admired her young golden's focus in the ring, and they had had a clean run.

She nodded proudly. "Gunny is one of the most honest dogs I've ever met. There's nothing he wouldn't do for Ginny, and he'll get his title this weekend. First time out."

I thought that might be a little optimistic, but

smiled encouragingly.

"Maude has fine dogs," Aggie added. "That's why I wanted to use one in my breeding program. I got four champions out of that litter."

I said, "I'll be sure to tell her." But the chances were that Maude already knew the history of any dog in which her kennel name had been involved. She'd been my father's clerk for thirty years and her propensity for meticulous recordkeeping had carried over into the world of dogs.

Aggie chuckled and confirmed my thoughts with, "She knows. We keep up with each other's dogs. In fact, that's why I'm glad to see you here. Maude's line has produced some solid working dogs, and I hear your Cisco has a pretty good start on a career in search and rescue himself. Ginny's moving to Boulder next month, and she's been talking about training Gunny for avalanche search and rescue when she gets out there. I know she'll want to talk to you about it, since Cisco and Gunny are practically cousins."

I started to protest that I didn't know anything about avalanche dogs when Miles, one of the most social people I know and an annoyingly efficient multitasker, glanced up from text-messaging and invited, "Why don't you and your daughter have dinner with us tonight? The hotel dining room isn't bad. Miles Young," he added, stretching across me to offer his hand. "Not her husband."

Aggie shook his hand, pleased to accept the invitation, and I smiled a little weakly. Of course I'm always up for spending time with another golden retriever lover, but I'd kind of been looking forward to room service that night. Room service was, in fact, the best thing about traveling with dogs.

We chatted a little more, and I learned that both Aggie and her daughter were part of the host club for this event. Miles held up his phone to me, which displayed a picture of Melanie standing in front of the Washington Monument, and said, "Mel says hi." I told him to tweet hi back from Raine and Cisco, and the next group was called.

"Summer is up," called the gate steward. "Flame on deck!"

"Flame?" I said, leaning forward to get a better look at the intense little border collie who was next in line. "As in Neil Kellog and Flame? I didn't know they were going to be here!"

"Who are they?" Miles asked.

In the time it took him to ask the question, Summer broke her start-line stay, completely destroying her handler's two-obstacle lead out, sailed over the first jump, took a wrong course, knocked over the bars on the next two jumps, and tore into the tunnel backward. The whistle sounded when she emerged from the tunnel and jumped over the seesaw without touching it, and a ring crew flooded in to repair the damage.

"Neil is last year's national champion, that's all," I told Miles, "with his other dog, Bryte. *And* he won the Standard Cup two years in a row. Bryte's the fastest dog in the Southeast, and her sister, Flame, isn't far behind." I reached for his phone. "I'll bet you anything she's the next champion. Let me borrow your phone. I want to video this."

He turned a shoulder to me, eyes on the screen. "Hold on. Downloading from Belgium. Where's yours?"

"Back at the camp in Cisco's crate."

Now he looked up. "You left your phone in a dog crate? What for?"

"Because that's where you keep important stuff at a dog show."

Now his expression turned incredulous. "Did you leave your purse there, too?"

I arched an eyebrow. "My mother always said all a lady needs when she's with a gentleman is a lipstick and a twenty." I snatched the phone from him. "After all, you're paying for dinner, right?" I turned on the camera function and zoomed in. "Who knows when I'll get another chance to video a run like this. People pay hundreds of dollars to go to one of Neil's workshops."

"Of course you've heard the stories about him," offered Aggie, lowering her voice a little.

The dog show circuit abounds with stories about everyone, but you know what they say: If you can't say anything good about somebody, come sit by me. I was no more immune to gossip than anyone else, and I turned to her, immediately interested. "What?"

"He dopes his dogs," she confided.

There are a few respectable breeders in this world, those who are dedicated to improving the health, temperament, and function of their chosen breed, who monitor the welfare of their puppies for a lifetime and take full responsibility for making sure they always have the best possible homes, care, and training. These people aren't in it for the money, but for the love of the dog, and they deserve our respect. Maude believed Aggie Connor was just such a breeder, or she never would have loaned her one of her dogs for stud. Whatever she had to say, therefore, automatically gained credibility with me.

To a point, of course. The thing to remember about competition, any competition, is that everyone has an agenda.

Miles said, "Steroids? For dogs?"

I shook my head impatiently. "Not steroids."

"Thyroid supplement," supplied Aggie.

I explained, "It amps your dog up. Not exactly illegal, but not very smart, either. The dog's heart can literally explode."

"Steroids for dogs," Miles repeated.

I started to argue, but then admitted, "I guess so. Kind of."

He tilted his head toward me skeptically. "You're sure Vegas isn't involved in this?"

I ignored him, studying beautiful Flame and her tall, wiry handler. "I don't believe it," I said. "Look at her focus. Besides, who would take chances with a dog that good?"

Aggie shrugged. "People will do all kinds of things for money, and this year's Standard Cup is worth a hundred grand. They're only inviting MACHs, you know, and Neil's a shoo-in with either Flame or Bryte. He only needs one more double-Q on each of them."

Miles said, "What's a MACH?"

"Master agility champion," I said. "It's as high as you can go in the sport, and not many dogs make it that far."

Miles raised an eyebrow. "A hundred grand, huh? I thought you said there weren't any cash prizes."

"I meant in competitive agility. Standard is a pet food company," I explained, "and the Standard Cup isn't a sanctioned agility trial. Every year they put together a trial with the top competitors from each region, and the winner gets a big silver cup and a check. ESPN usually carries it, and last year Animal Planet did a whole series of shows about the dogs that were competing. *The Road to the Standard Cup*."

He nodded approvingly. "Now that makes sense. I knew somebody had to be making money somewhere."

I spared him a disparaging glance. "It's always about money with you."

"Sweetheart," he assured me, and gave Aggie a smiling wink, "it's all about money with everything."

Sometimes I really wonder why I even like him.

"Flame is up," called the gate steward as the

crew scurried from the ring.

I pulled Cisco between my knees, crossed my ankles in front of him, and wrapped his leash securely around my palm, focusing the camera phone with the other hand. There was about to be a lot of shouting. "Watch this," I told Miles. "They're amazing. And if I had any money, I *would* bet on her."

"I'd take a piece of that, girlfriend," said Aggie.

Neil stepped to the start line, slipped Flame's collar and leash over her head, and put her in a sit-stay. He walked confidently away from her, past the first two jumps, past the chute, past the tire, to the jump spiral, a five-obstacle lead out. I held my breath, but the little dog sat like a statue, her eyes boring holes into his back, every muscle in her body coiled to spring. He turned, made eye contact with his dog, and raised his hand. Almost before he completed the motion she had taken two jumps, the chute, and another jump in the precise correct sequence and was by his side, both of them in motion. The crowd was on its feet, cheering them on, as he pivoted to guide her through the spiral, over the bar jump, up and over the A-frame— perfect contacts!—to the pause table for a flawless five-second stay. He never said a word. It was as though they were telepathically linked. I'd never seen anything like it. A one-eighty into the weave poles, the seesaw, the broad jump, then into a blind cross around the A-frame and into the tunnel. With only four obstacles to go, the unthinkable happened. Coming out of the pivot that had sent his dog into the tunnel and swinging the opposite way to meet her on the other side, Neil lost his balance and went down in the dirt. A collective cry of dismay went up from the spectators.

Flame came flying out of the tunnel with her handler nowhere in sight. But this is what makes a championship team. Before his dog exited the tunnel Neil called, "Over, over, walk it!" He couldn't see Flame and she couldn't see him, but he was guiding her through the course and she was doing what she was trained to do. He regained his feet just as she touched the down contact zone on the dog walk, but he was still three obstacles behind her and there was no way he could catch up now. Amazingly, Flame looked as though she would take the last two jumps on her own, and we were all on our feet, cheering in anticipation as Flame raced toward the finish to the kind of applause and cheers usually reserved for Olympic athletes breaking a world record. We were all competitors, of course, and we all wanted the blue ribbon, but when you see something like that you start to understand why people say it really is all about how you play the game.

And then the most astonishing thing happened. As she made the turn toward the last jump and the finish line, the border collie stopped so suddenly that a cloud of dust flew up around her. She spun and barked—a typical sign of frustration in this high-strung breed—then ran back over the jump she had just taken to return to Neil and leapt into his arms. A groan of disappointment rose up from the crowd as the judge blew her whistle to indicate an elimination. I lowered the camera in disbelief. They were out.

"I guess that means they didn't win," observed Miles, holding out his hand for the phone.

"What a shame," exclaimed Aggie, settling back into her seat. "She must have spooked after he fell."

"I guess," I murmured. I returned Miles's phone to him absently, watching Neil limp out of the ring with Flame in his arms. "It's just that…"

"What?" Miles, who was learning to read me too well, glanced at me curiously.

I shook my head. "Nothing. I thought I saw something, but it's silly."

"Oh, look," said Aggie, waving happily to someone below as the ring crew came in to set up the equipment for the next class. "There's Ginny."

"I'm going to help set up the ring," I said, handing Cisco's leash to Miles. "Stay right here. Keep your eye on him. And no food."

Miles tucked his phone back into his pocket and held up his hand in a solemn promise.

"And don't let Cisco play with the other dogs."

"I won't."

I started down the stairs. "And don't let anyone pet him."

He gave me a long-suffering look. "Maybe Cisco and I should just wait in the car."

You see, if I had an RV I wouldn't have this problem.

"Just stay here." I hurried down to the ring.

CHAPTER THREE

THREE

Hansonville, North Carolina

Twenty-eight hours before the shooting

The sign on the door said "Sheriff" in bold, stenciled letters and below that "Buck Lawson," written in black marker on a piece of poster paper taped in place. It was just another reminder, as if he needed one, that he wasn't the real sheriff, and his place in this office was only temporary. Some days that suited him just fine. Other days, like today, it got under his skin like a bad rash.

Buck was currently serving out the unexpired term of Roe Bleckley, who'd been elected sheriff of Hanover County nine consecutive times and whose well-worn boots, to put it mildly, were hard to fill. Roe had retired after a heart attack and it surprised no one that Buck had been tagged to step into the job, not only because he was the senior man on the force, but because, having been married to Roe's niece Raine for over ten years, he was practically family. The fact that his marriage to Raine had been over long before Roe's unexpected retirement hadn't figured into most people's thinking. Neither, if truth be told, had the possibility that Buck might not want the job.

Buck Lawson was a good law officer, but he hated being sheriff. He hated working fourteen-hour days and spending twelve of them behind a desk. He hated drawing up duty rosters and filling out payroll forms. He hated attending budget meetings. And he hated opening piece after piece of mail addressed to "R.O. Bleckley, Sheriff."

"Rosie!" He ripped open yet another envelope addressed to the former sheriff, leaned toward the open door, and shouted more loudly, "Rosie!"

Her reply came distantly over the buzz and hum of activity from the outer office. "Yes, your lordship!"

Rosie's official title was Head Dispatcher, but she'd been with the Sheriff's Department even longer than Buck and was the only person on board who really knew how everything worked. The budget, as Buck discovered all too soon, didn't allow for an office manager, so Roe had solved the problem by changing Rosie's job description, but not her title. It was that kind of creative thinking that was sorely missed around here by everyone, including Buck.

She appeared at the door, a middle-aged woman with a poufy faded-brown hairdo that hadn't changed in twenty years and too much eye makeup. She wore a wireless telephone headset in one ear and a pair of glasses pushed into her hair. "You bellowed?" she inquired politely.

"Sorry," he muttered. His former desk had been only steps from hers, and it had been easy to call over to her when he needed something. He couldn't get used to being stuck back here in the middle of a hallway with a door between him and the department he was supposed to be running. "Did you call Roe to come pick up his mail?"

"I did. He said he'd stop by after lunch."

Most of the mail that came through the office was official business that Buck would end up handling anyway, but he kept an ongoing stack of personal notices, magazines, brochures and the like addressed to Roe. The man had been in office for thirty years, and it was starting to look as though it would take at least that long to get his address changed on all those mailing lists.

Buck frowned a little as he glanced over the contents of the most recent letter. "You know anything about a felon by the name of Jeremiah Berman?"

"Can't say that I do," she replied. "But then, I know so many felons."

"I wonder why the pardons and paroles board would be notifying Roe about his release."

"Sounds routine to me. He must have put the guy away."

"No, it says here, 'At your request, we are notifying you…'" He gave a little grunt and put the letter aside—in his pile, not Roe's. "See what you can find out, will you?"

"Sure thing. Do you want me to call the—" He could tell by the way she broke off that she had been about to say "the sheriff." It was a common slip, and it didn't even bother him anymore.

"Just pull the file," he suggested, saving her the embarrassment of correcting herself.

"Will do." She started to leave and then turned back. "By the way, did you see the election forms I left on your desk?"

"Yeah, I saw them."

"Did you get a chance to fill them out?"

"Not yet."

"The deadline for filing is Monday, you know."

"I know."

"Do you want me to fill them out for you?"

"No, that's okay."

She hesitated, looked as though she wanted to say something else, but settled on, "Well, give me a holler when you're finished. I can run them down to the county clerk's office in a jiff."

"Yeah, okay. Thanks."

"Because the deadline's Monday."

"Got it."

"What deadline is that, young lady?" a familiar voice came from behind her, and Rosie broke into a broad smile as she turned.

"Afternoon, Sheriff," she said and didn't even bother to correct herself this time. "We were just talking about you."

"My ears were burning."

Roe was a round, balding man with an easy disposition and a quick smile. He'd lost a little weight since the doctor and his wife had forced him into a heart-healthy diet, but the most striking change in his appearance over the past year was the simple absence of a uniform. These days he spent most of his time trying to coordinate a volunteer cold-case squad for the neighboring mountain communities, and his uniform was typically jeans and a sweater. Even Buck sometimes had to blink before he recognized his former boss without his khakis.

Roe came into the office, and before Rosie could settle down for a nice chat with her former boss, Buck reminded her, "You want to see about that file?"

She looked puzzled for a moment and then remembered. "Right on it."

Roe said, "So how's everything in the law-and-order game?"

"Understaffed, overworked, underpaid." Buck picked up the stack of mail and handed it to him.

"Sounds about right." Roe took the mail and glanced through it without interest. "Finding plenty of spare time for all that paperwork, are you?"

"Not by half." Buck got up and crossed to the coffee maker on a small table next to the door—

perhaps the only perk of the job. He poured a cup and offered it to Roe, who shook his head.

"Guess that's why you haven't gotten around to filing the election forms yet," Roe observed.

Buck ignored that and took the coffee cup back to his desk. "Say, Roe, what do you know about a felon named..." He took up the letter from the pardons and parole board and glanced at it. "Berman?"

"Not a thing that I can recall."

Buck handed Roe the letter and watched the other man's face change as he read it. It wasn't a dramatic change—just a flicker of recognition, a passing shade of concern, and then, perhaps the most telling sign of all, a deliberate smoothing of his features into neutral. His only comment was, "Huh."

"Did you send him up?" Buck pressed.

"Never met the man."

"It's not like they were releasing him back into our neck of the woods. Says there his last known residence was Georgia."

"So it does." He glanced again at the letter and couldn't quite hide the small frown that creased his brow as he read the date. "Looks like he got out almost three weeks ago. When did this get here, anyhow?"

"Just today. I guess they get backed up on paperwork up at the parole board, too." He looked at his former boss intensely. "What's going on, Roe?"

"Nothing," Roe said, folding the letter. "Probably nothing." Then he looked at Buck. "Listen, if you don't mind a piece of advice…"

Buck managed to keep a straight face. Since he'd taken over the job, he had gotten more advice from Roe on how to do it than he'd counted on, asked for, or needed.

"You need to hire yourself another deputy," Roe said.

"I've been thinking about it."

"You've been down two since you took over the job. You've got the budget."

"Yeah, I know." Buck frowned thoughtfully as he sipped his coffee. "Mind if I ask you something?" Without waiting for a reply, he went on. "What do you think about bringing Wyn back?"

Roe's silence was about what he had expected and the only answer he needed.

Wyn had been Buck's partner back when Buck was still a deputy and Roe was in charge. They'd ridden together for three years before they realized their feelings for each other went beyond professional, and even though Buck had been separated from Raine at the time, it was their involvement that led to the final divorce. When he took over as sheriff, Wyn voluntarily left the force, and town, for a security job an hour away. Since then they'd been driving back and forth to see each other on weekends and after shift, and Buck was more than ready to make some changes.

He said, "She's thinking about moving back to town."

"Oh yeah? Where's she going to be living?"

"With me."

Roe's expression remained detached. "Reckon you all will be getting married, then."

Buck couldn't prevent a small flash of alarm, even though he half-suspected the comment was just Roe's way of needling him. He said carefully, "I can't say we've gone that far in our thinking."

"Well, maybe you ought to. She's a good woman. A good woman deserves somebody who'll put a little thought into the matter before asking her to turn her life upside down."

Buck knew he was treading on uncertain ground. He had, after all, married and divorced Roe's only niece, not once, but twice, and he imagined there had been more than one heated conversation behind closed doors about that. So he said, "Mostly right now I'm just wondering what the rest of the boys would think if she came back to work here."

Roe nodded, his expression carefully concealed. "She was a good deputy. Well-liked on the force."

"Yeah, she was."

"I reckon they'd just be glad to have their days off back."

"That's what I was thinking."

"But it's a small town, Buck. Something like this… well, it's not going to win you the election."

Buck blew out a breath. "Right."

"I'd think about it if I was you."

"Right."

"Meantime…" Roe tilted his head meaningfully toward the desk. "Get busy and file those forms."

"Yeah. Right."

It wasn't until after he was gone that Buck realized Roe had taken the letter from the parole board with him.

And why shouldn't he? After all, the letter had been addressed to him.

Sheriff Bleckley.

Putting on an agility trial is hard work and the sponsoring club never has enough volunteers so I like to help out whenever I can. But that's not the only reason I'm among the first to lend a hand when it comes time to set up the ring for a new course. For one thing, volunteering to help guarantees acceptance into most trials, and in a trial as popular as this one, that's a huge advantage. In addition, it not only offers a sneak preview of the course to come; it also gives me extra time to familiarize myself with the ring and plan my strategy in my head. I could definitely use every advantage I could get, but that was only part of the reason I was anxious to help out this time. Neil and Flame were still on the floor, and being the naturally curious person that I am, I hoped to get the inside scoop on their last run before they got away.

He was in an intense conversation with a young woman with her dark ponytail threaded through the back of her baseball cap like mine and gorgeous legs that were prominently displayed in white shorts and high-tech running shoes. Reticence has never been one of my problems, so I put a big smile on my face and approached confidently, and by the time I realized they were in the midst of a furious argument, it was too late to alter my course.

I heard the girl say shortly, "Do you think I'm blind? I saw what you did and you're not going to get away with it. And if you think I'm going to stand by and let you ruin Flame's career—"

"You've got bigger problems than Flame's career if you think I'm stupid enough to believe that's all you're worried about," he returned tightly. "I don't play by your rules anymore, sweetheart, just in case you haven't figured that out yet."

"We've got a contract, big boy," she retorted in a tone thick with anger, "and you know I've got the chops to enforce it. If you screw with me I'll have everything you own, including your reputation."

"Look at me. I'm trembling," he returned. Red spots of anger started to appear on his neck. "I ran her, didn't I? I gave it my best and fullest effort, to quote your precious contract, and if you have any doubts you just ask any one of the spectators that were cheering in the stands. It was an accident, and nothing you can do will prove otherwise." His smile was cold. "These things happen. It's all part of the game."

She said lowly, "You fool. You have no idea what you've done."

To which he replied, "I know exactly what I've done, and now you know what I'm capable of, you selfish—" Then he noticed me and stopped abruptly, looking both annoyed and embarrassed. There was nothing I could do but pretend I had heard nothing.

"Great run," I congratulated him brightly. "That silent handling is unbelievable. What a shame about the finish. What happened?"

The girl spun and stalked away, and the eyes that followed her had enough venom in them to choke a snake. With an effort, he dragged his attention back to me. "Refusal," he said briefly.

I forced a laugh. "Yeah, I saw. She was going straight for the finish line, though. I could've sworn she was going to make it. She's such an incredible dog."

The fastest way to any dog lover's heart is to compliment his dog, so it didn't surprise me to see Neil's expression soften. "Yes, she is," he agreed, glancing down fondly at the little dog at his side.

She sat at his side with her eyes fixed upon him with the same rapt attention she had displayed at the start line. "She probably got spooked when I fell."

"But she took half the course after that. It was the most amazing thing I've ever seen. It wasn't until she was almost at the finish line that she turned back. I wonder what happened."

He shrugged. "I don't know and she's not talking. Anyway, there's always tomorrow."

"That's the good thing about a three-day," I agreed. "I hope your leg is better."

He winced, as though being reminded of the injury brought back pain he'd forgotten, and he reached down to rub his knee. "Yeah, I twisted my knee a little. I'll ice it. It'll be okay."

"If not," I suggested with a grin, "you could just stand at the start line and tell her what to do."

It took him a moment to respond, and then it was with an absent smile that told me I'd overstayed my welcome. His eyes were watching someone over my shoulder, and I didn't have to look beyond the cold anger in them to guess who it was. He said, "I guess. Excuse me, will you?"

He dropped his hand to his side with a gesture that was so quick and so small even I had trouble seeing it, and Flame fell into a perfect heel as he strode away, following the girl with the ponytail.

I ran to join the other volunteers in the ring, got my instructions and my course map, and paired with Ginny to set up the jumps. She was a cute girl in her late twenties with short blond hair and a personality as chatty as her mother's. I introduced myself and congratulated her on a clean run.

"Gunny's just starting out in agility," she admitted, "but he *is* good, isn't he? Of course, he'll never be another Flame, but then I'm no Neil Kellog. Have you ever taken one of his workshops? He's brilliant. He has his dogs trained to these hand signals he learned in the army. I've never seen anything like it. Every obstacle has a number and he holds up that number of fingers to send them over. Of course he uses voice commands, too, for some of the dogs, and in an emergency, like he did just now. Is number three a wing jump or a broad jump?"

For a moment I thought she was still talking about hand signals, but then I glanced at the course map and replied, "Wing."

We dragged the two supports into place and moved on. "I couldn't believe she refused the finish line," Ginny went on. "And then to back-jump? I'll bet Neil was mad. He always plays to win, and usually does, too. Win, that is. But to not even qualify?" She gave a small shake of her head. "Crazy. On the other hand..." She brightened. "That opens up the field for somebody else to win high in trial." Like I said, she was as chatty as her mother.

"He seemed to be taking it pretty well, though," I observed, dragging the opening of the tunnel to face the A-frame. "It was the woman who was mad. Who is she, anyway?"

Ginny set the number cone beside the tunnel. "That's his girlfriend, Marcie. Ex-girlfriend, I should say. They're both in our agility club. And she should be mad. Neil's running both Flame and Bryte this weekend, but Flame's her dog, and she was counting on that MACH."

"Oh yeah?" I said. "I've never seen anyone but Neil run her."

"They co-own Flame and most of the other dogs," said Ginny. "She's the breeder. He's the trainer. I think she's always resented it a little that Neil got all the glory, and of course, now that they're not together anymore, it'll be a mess trying to assign custody of the dogs."

To anyone but a dog person, that might sound

47

strange. But in the case of competition dogs, even more than conformation show dogs, this was serious business.

"She said something about a contract."

Ginny gave a little snort of amusement as she set a bar on the ground between two stanchions at the number six cone. "Doesn't surprise me a bit. She's a lawyer, and she's probably got Neil tied up six ways from Sunday. He'll be lucky if he walks away from this with his shirt. She probably only got together with Neil in the first place for his training skills." She grinned and offered, before I could ask, "She's president of the agility club, so naturally it's all been a big scandal. Everyone's gossiping."

"Well," I said, "the season's just started. There's plenty of time for Flame to get her MACH."

"Not if they want to qualify for the Standard Cup," Ginny said. "Entries have to be in by May first. And there isn't another sanctioned trial in the region before then."

"Wow," I said. "I hope he's able to run tomorrow, then."

And that was when I remembered something odd. When Neil had first gotten up from his fall, he favored his right leg. But when he walked away from me just now, he favored his left.

Odd.

I was feeling pretty confident about the course. There were only one tricky part requiring a front cross between the tire jump and the A-frame, but my nemesis and Cisco's, the dog walk, was the first obstacle, and I knew if we could get that out of the way we'd be okay. I'd checked the schedule, and we were in the first group. This was good news and bad news. The good news was that the course would still be fresh in my mind and there'd be no time for nerves to build up in me or boredom to build up in Cisco. The bad news was there would be very little time for warming up.

It was a big group, and the judge's last group of the morning, so she didn't waste any time as she called us all in for the briefing. In the novice classes the judges usually go out of their way to be welcoming and friendly, but as you move up through the levels they figure you don't need quite as much encouragement to stay in the game. They do, however, generally take a moment to welcome the competitors at the beginning and wish them luck at the end. This one did neither. She informed us tersely of the set course time, reminded us to be on deck when the dog ahead of us reached the broad jump, and reminded us briefly of the elimination faults. She gave us six minutes to walk the course— not five, not ten—and that was it. We were a pretty frantic group trotting around the obstacles, waving our arms and muttering to ourselves, plotting out our strategies in our heads. I was happier than ever to have had the extra time in the ring that setting up the course allowed me.

I took Cisco for a quick potty walk, turned my pockets inside out—a superstitious habit I have, just to make sure I don't accidentally walk into the ring with liver treats or a training clicker in my pocket—blew a kiss to Miles, and got into line with the other dogs in my jump height. I have another superstition, which involves a few quiet moments with Cisco before a run, visualizing the course in my head and whispering the commands out loud to Cisco. My friend Sonny, who claims to be an animal communicator of sorts, says when I do this Cisco actually memorizes the course. Given the number of off-course faults he generally racks up, this seems unlikely. But any sports psychologist will tell you the most powerful way to improve your game is to visualize a perfect run, and saying the commands out loud not only helps me remember them in order, but hopefully puts Cisco in training mode. This time, however, my hope was moot. Cisco had eyes for no one but Brinkley, who was two dogs ahead of us in line, and even I had to laugh when Brinkley began his run and Cisco barked every time he made a jump, just as though he was cheering him on.

I'd been working on Cisco's start-line stay all winter and it was the one thing of which I was fairly confident—particularly now that Brinkley was safely out of sight and no one else with whom Cisco would rather be was there to distract him. Being able to leave your dog at the start line and meet him somewhere along the course is a huge advantage when you have a fast dog who operates on visual cues, because no two-legged human can hope to keep up with a four-legged dog, and it was vital Cisco be able to see me at all times. I tossed his leash to the gate steward and put him in a sit facing the first obstacle. His brown-eyed gaze was focused alertly on me as I strode toward the elevated bridge of the dog walk, passed it, and turned to face him. With every step I repeated, *Stay, stay, stay...* in my head. My spirits soared when I turned and saw he was still where I left him. Already, the taste of victory was sweet on my tongue. Our first run of the season was going to be a winner, I could feel it.

But this was the tricky part. I raised my hand to cue him to readiness, but before I could even draw a breath, he took off like a shot toward the dog walk, leaving me scrambling to catch up. I hate it when that happens.

Of course, a less sanguine handler would be completely thrown by something like that, but the advantage of having tried—and failed—so many times for a clean run was that I was prepared for the fact that anything that could go wrong, would go wrong. I dived for the dog walk and met Cisco there as he raced across the top plank, guiding him with my shoulder, calling, "Easy! Easy!" as he began his descent. And, yes!—all four paws in the yellow contact zone—and I shouted, "Over!" as he tore off toward a series of ninety-degree jumps. I did a rear cross at the tunnel, because Cisco had knocked me off my feet too many times barreling out of the tunnel when I tried to meet him in front. I cut behind him toward the tire, and when he was three quarters of the way through the tunnel, I called, "Tire!" He turned toward the sound of my voice when he emerged and sailed through the tire like a dolphin through a hoop. Am I good or what?

The pause table was the third obstacle from the end, which is kind of a mean trick. The dog is flying high on adrenaline—not to mention the handler—when suddenly he's required to come to a screeching halt on the table, stay perfectly still for five seconds, and then take off like lightning again on cue. For a dog like Cisco, whose impulse control is not exactly legendary and whose attention span is often measured in microseconds, this can be risky business, to say the least. I didn't dare take my eyes off him. I didn't breathe. I didn't move a muscle as I focused on the countdown: *Four, three...*

And then I heard a familiar bark from outside the ring. Cisco's ears went up; his head swiveled toward Brinkley. *No, no, no...*

"Two, go!" called the counter, and before the "o" in "go" died, I shouted, "Here!"

The trick to winning at agility is to outthink your dog. It takes a dog about two seconds to process a verbal command— which is actually faster than it takes a human—so if he's running at 2.25 yards per second, you have to give the command for the obstacle at least five yards before he has to set his course toward it. This means you often have to give the commands faster than your dog can run. Sometimes that's possible; sometimes it's not. Either way, it all happens in a blur.

The last two obstacles were straight-line jumps leading to the finish line, a piece of cake except for the fact that the jumps were positioned behind the table. "Here" was the one word I knew with a fair amount of certainty that Cisco would respond to, even with the temptation of his best friend's bark to distract him, so I called, "Here!" and, "Over!" in the same breath. Cisco sprang off the table, racing toward me like a jet rocket, just as I spun around to direct him toward the jumps. One of us miscalculated.

He barreled into me full speed, cracking his forehead against my nose before bouncing off. I saw stars. Blood sprayed the sand, and I went down like the proverbial sack of lead.

CHAPTER FOUR

Twenty-two hours before the shooting

Buck got tied up on a call with one of the commissioners, and he had a conference call with the state police at two. Just before three o'clock, Rosie brought in the schedule of court appearances and a stack of forms for him to initial, which he did without glancing at them. "Did you find the file on that Berman fellow?"

"It was in the basement, from 1993 when the case was closed, before we started putting everything on the computer. You know, if you could get the commissioners to authorize just two clerks, we could start scanning some of that stuff in."

"Yeah, that and other dreams." He scrawled his last "BL" and glanced up at her. "Well? Where is it?"

"The sheriff—that is, Mr. Bleckley took it with

him."

He stared at her. "He did what?'

"That's what you wanted it for, isn't it? I mean, I didn't think to ask… I just figured…"

Buck bit down hard on his temper. His back teeth ached with the effort. He pushed up abruptly from the desk and strode toward the door.

"Where are you going?"

"Lunch."

"But it's almost three o'clock!"

"You think I don't know that?"

"Buck…" She sounded worried. "Did I do something wrong?"

He sucked in a breath as he looked back at her and then compressed his lips tightly against the words that wanted to be blurted. In the end all he said was a terse, "Next time, ask." And, because she was still in the room, he didn't even get the satisfaction of slamming the door on his way out.

Buck had always found that it took less energy to let his anger go than to hold on to it, and if he got mad about everything that went wrong in this office, he wouldn't have time to do anything but get mad. By the time he walked the three blocks to Meg's Diner, he'd calmed considerably. Roe's SUV was parked in front, just as he figured it would be, which saved him a trip out to the country.

This late in the day Meg wasn't officially serving, but she looked up from wiping the counter when he came in and called, "Afternoon, Buck. Don't tell me you're just now getting around to lunch."

"I'm afraid so, Meg. What've you got left over for a poor starving lawman?"

The place was nearly empty. John Williams, from the bank, was chatting over coffee with Preacher Barton, and a couple of women at a window table lingered over pie. Roe was in a booth, and he looked up, unsurprised, when Buck came in.

"How about I whip you up a club sandwich and a fresh batch of fries?" Meg offered. "I've got some blueberry pie, too."

"Meg, I swear, I'm going to marry you some day."

Meg, who was easily twice his age, winked at him and replied, "I'm not going to wait forever, you handsome thing," as she disappeared into the kitchen. Buck made his way over to Roe, stopping to speak to John and the preacher and nodding pleasantly toward the women at the window table. They smiled back at him.

He slid into the booth opposite Roe. "You know you can go to jail for stealing official government documents."

Roe leaned back against the seat with a small frown. He closed the file and pushed it toward Buck. "I just wanted to see if it made any more sense now than it did back then."

Buck turned a couple of pages. "Looks pretty straightforward to me. Felony murder, pled to second degree, thirty years, served twenty. No ballistics?"

Roe shook his head. "We never found the bullet."

"Two eyewitnesses."

"Yeah."

They both knew that in the case of violent crimes eyewitness reports could be among the least reliable evidence of all.

Buck glanced through the reports submitted by the arresting officer in Georgia and flipped over to the suspect's statement. Halfway through, he smothered a mirthless snort of laughter. "If I was going to try to alibi out, I believe I'd come up with something better than I was on my way home from selling crack to Smokey Beardsley at the time of the robbery." He glanced up at Roe. "Checked out, did it?"

Roe rubbed his nose, his lips quirking dryly. "About like you'd expect. Keep reading."

Meg placed a mug of coffee in front of Buck and topped off Roe's from the pot she carried. Buck thanked her and she said, "It'll just be another minute on those fries, hon." The room had already begun to fill with the aroma of hot grease.

Meg went back to the kitchen, calling good-bye to the two ladies as the bell over the door announced their departure. Buck read on, paused, and read it again. He glanced at Roe. "Hit and run, huh? Did an accident report ever come in?"

The other man shook his head. "He says it was just a fender bender, no injuries. Maybe no damage. The other party might not have wanted to turn it in to their insurance, or might not have wanted it on their record for whatever reason. Could have been some kid in daddy's car..." He shrugged. "Lots of reasons."

"So he drove up from Georgia about five o'clock that afternoon, stopped at the Cash-n-Carry for gas and kept the receipt, spent an hour or two visiting his good buddy Smokey, and was sixty miles away, sideswiping a green sedan, by nine-o'clock, when the robbery happened. No ideas on the other driver?"

Roe shook his head. "He said he didn't see the driver, but swore up and down he could identify the passenger. There's a description there."

Buck glanced at it. "Pretty generic. Still, if he could've found whoever was in the other car, that would have corroborated his timeline. And with everything else circumstantial..." He shrugged. "I can't see him serving time. I'm guessing you never found the other car?"

"Never looked," said Roe. "By the time we got around to it, he'd pled out."

Police matters in a small town never moved with quite the same efficiency that they did on television crime dramas. Buck flipped through the file once more, then looked up at Roe. "What am I missing here? Some passing cokehead commits armed robbery on his way home from dealing drugs, no other connections here... What made you put in a notification request? You got some reason to think he might come back here? What's special about this guy?"

Roe sipped his coffee. "Yeah, I wondered the same thing at the time. I wasn't the one who wanted to keep tabs on him. It was Jon."

Buck frowned a little. "Judge Stockton?"

"He was the judge on the case."

Buck thought about that while Meg set a tall club sandwich and a steaming plate of fries in front of him. "You boys need anything else right now? I've got some sweet tea if you get tired of that coffee."

"Thanks, Meg, it looks great."

Buck reached for the bottle of ketchup on the table as Meg departed, and he said, "So did this dude Berman threaten him or what?"

"Not in open court. That would've gone on the record. He just came to me real quiet like a day or two later and asked would I do him a favor and let him know when the man got out."

"Wonder why," said Buck.

"I asked. Never did get an answer."

"Maybe he knew the family."

"Maybe."

Buck ate in silence for a while. Then he said, "So do you think you got the right man?"

Roe leaned back again in his seat and released a quiet breath. "I don't know." His tone was heavy. "At the time I did. You know how it is. We get a handful of violent crimes a year around here, most of them drug-related. We put it out over the wire and within the hour the Georgia boys picked up a

DUI matching his description, same kind of damage to the front fender, a wad of cash and a thirty-eight in the glove box... Looked like a wrap to me. You don't go chasing after the maybes when you've got a suspect sitting in your cell. Maybe that's not right. But that's the way it is."

Buck chewed thoughtfully. "You said 'at the time' you thought you had the right man. Something happen to change your mind?"

He hesitated, then shook his head, frowning at the file on the table between them. "Nope," he said. "I didn't see a thing in that file to make me think we got the wrong man." He drained his cup and stood. "Or that we got the right one, either."

Buck swallowed quickly. "Hey, wait a minute. That's it? Judge Stockton wanted to keep an eye on this guy. He must've had his reasons. Don't you think we should do some kind of follow-up?"

"I don't know what. Jon is the one who wanted to keep up with him, and he's dead. I guess his reasons died with him."

"Maybe." Buck put down the sandwich and opened the front flap of the file again. "But I think I'll give his parole officer a call anyway."

"You do what you think's best." Roe smiled and clapped him on the shoulder as he passed.

"That's why they're paying you the sheriff's money, son, not me."

CHAPTER FIVE

Twenty-one hours before the shooting

My mother used to say that you can learn more from playing games than from anything else in life, as long as you pay attention. For example, from chess you learn patience, from tennis you learn how to keep your eye on the ball, from soccer and basketball you learn no one wins by himself, and from football you learn good financial planning because your career will very likely be short. I've learned a lot from running agility, but perhaps the most important thing is not to give up until you cross the finish line, because in this game it really isn't over until it's over.

The average person might think that once your dog has knocked you off your feet and given you a bloody nose the game is over and, all things considered, that might be a good time to give up. But the average person, not having competed with Cisco for almost two years, would have no way of knowing that we'd been in much worse spots than that. I barely hit the ground before I sprang up again, shouting Cisco on. Cisco took the last two jumps and crossed the finish line on his way to answer Brinkley's tempting call, and that's how I came now to hold a blue ribbon in my hand. Not red, not green, but *blue*. In dogs, as in life, you don't always have to be the best to win; sometimes all it takes is for everyone else to be worse than you are. And sometimes the gods just smile on you. Cisco and I had taken first place in our jump height, and I suspect the reason was a combination of the two.

"It's probably not broken," Miles said, gently placing a paper towel-wrapped plastic bag of ice across the bridge of my nose, "but you're going to have a shiner. Are you sure you don't want to go to the emergency room?"

I just grinned at him, hugging my furry golden hero with one arm while I admired the blue ribbon I held in the other hand. "Did you see him? He was a magic dog! Like lightning! Did I tell you what our time was? 58.3! And that's with the course fault, which means he really ran it in 53.3 seconds! What do you think of that?"

"I think you may have a concussion. You sound delirious."

I laughed and hugged Cisco again. Cisco obligingly swiped my face with his tongue and grinned at me proudly. He knew he'd done good.

Miles sank into a camp chair beside me and scooped out a soft drink from the cooler. We'd returned to our temporary day campsite in the shady open-air livestock barn, where I'd snagged one of the private stalls by being there before the gates opened that morning. The stalls were clean and concrete floored, big enough for four or five dogs and a couple of people in each one, along with crates, coolers, camp chairs, and all the other paraphernalia required for a dog show. And, most importantly, they were gated, so Cisco could wander around free while we were there. It was almost as good as having an RV. Cisco's travel bag, with his training treats, toys, collapsible bowls, pick-up bags, a chamois square for drying muddy paws, and space blanket to serve as sunshade or wind block, plus a battery-operated fan in case the weather turned hot, sat atop his crate. Next to it was my travel bag, with sunblock, insect repellent, extra socks, a spare Golden Retriever Club of America sweatshirt, first aid kit, emergency shoelaces, and a couple protein bars. I never knew how long my day would last at one of these big trials, so it paid to come prepared.

Behind us was a big grassy field for exercising dogs, liberally dotted with waste cans and signs reminding people to pick up after their dogs. A couple of people were tossing flying discs or balls for their dogs; others were practicing attention exercises or sit-stays. At the edge of the field, minivans and SUVs were parked, most with their hatchback doors open and crated dogs inside. Some of the dogs were seasoned veterans who knew the value of conserving their energy; others, mostly border collies, passed the time in frantic barking.

"The first trial we ever competed in," I said happily, "Cisco ran half the course and then jumped in the ring steward's lap."

"I take it you're not supposed to do that."

"Not if you don't want to get disqualified. It's considered a major off-course." I ruffled Cisco's ears affectionately. "Last year I was running

Mischief when Cisco broke out of his crate and ran the entire course by himself. Fastest time of the day. Of course, he didn't exactly run the course the judge had laid out, and we were excused for the rest of the trial, but that's when I knew he really had a talent for agility. We've come a long way."

"Doesn't surprise me a bit." He popped the top on the soft drink and passed it to me, then took another for himself. "I always back the winner." He turned on his phone. "You looked really good," he added, "up until the crash. Do you want to see the video?"

I removed the ice pack from my face and leaned over to watch the video. It was pure poetry in motion up until, as Miles pointed out, the last five seconds or so. I couldn't help grinning as I relived our triumph and wincing when it got to the end. I knew it was only by the grace of God and the judge's good mood that the collision had resulted in a mere five points off for bad handling rather than an elimination, which is what I'd assumed the judge would call when I went down. If I hadn't gotten up and finished the course anyway, that's exactly what would have happened.

Miles pressed a button on the phone. "Just sent it to Mel. She wanted to know how Cisco did."

I dug in my travel bag for Cisco's brush. "Wait, you should send her a picture."

I was making it a point to chronicle our big weekend on Facebook and had already posted pictures of our arrival at the hotel, loading up the SUV, arriving at the fairgrounds, our crating area in the livestock barn, our practice jumps, and many of the dogs who were competing against us. I would post the picture of our blue ribbon double the size of the other photos, but Melanie deserved the first look.

Miles's phone chimed with a text message. He grinned as he read it, then held it out to me. Melanie texted: *Is Cisco okay?*

Spoken like a true dog person. I was the one crumpled on the ground in the video, but she was worried about my dog. I couldn't fault her for that. I finished brushing down Cisco, straightened my Air Bud cap, and picked up the blue ribbon. "Okay, send her this." He snapped the photo of me kneeling with my arm around Cisco, holding the blue ribbon in front of his chest and grinning around my puffy nose and purple eye like I'd just won Olympic gold, and sent it off to Washington. I said, "Send it to my phone, too. I want to put it on Facebook."

"Done. Both videos too."

"Thanks." I got up and leaned outside the half door of the stall to hang the ribbon from one of the overhead nails that were provided for that purpose. I saw that some of the other competitors had already accumulated four or five ribbons, and some of them had even brought banners with their dog's name or their kennel name emblazoned on them to hang over the stall entrance. Really, the lengths to which some people will go in this game... I wondered where I could get a banner with Cisco's name on it before tomorrow.

From where I stood I could see the parking area with its line of minivans and SUVS with the back hatches open, part of the dog walk area and play field, and the corner of the jumpers-with-weaves ring, which was empty now. In less than an hour, Cisco and I would be making our second and last run of the day in that very ring. I saw Brinkley and his handler, heading toward the field with a Frisbee, and waved. She waved back and called, "Congratulations!" and I returned, "Thanks!" I wasn't sure whether I should ask her to make sure to keep Brinkley out of sight during our next run or offer to pay her to stand with him at the finish line.

That was a joke, of course. I would never cheat

in agility.

But the thought, along with a glimpse of Neil Kellog's girlfriend, Marcie, taking one of her border collies out of a crate in the back of a minivan, reminded me of something that had been nagging at me all afternoon. I turned back. "Say, Miles…"

But his phone buzzed just then and he held up a finger as he glanced at the screen. "Need to get this one, babe."

I rolled my eyes—he knows I hate it when he calls me "babe"—and he answered, "Miles Young." He edged past me through the gate, brushing a kiss across my eyebrow as he did so, and took the call outside.

I made sure the gate was closed firmly behind him, settled Cisco down with a chew bone, and dug into my bag for my own phone. I sank back into my chair and enjoyed the video of our win one more time, then pulled up the other video Miles had sent. I watched Flame zip around the course as though she'd memorized it herself. I watched her stutter at the finish line and turn back, clearly frustrated, to return to her handler. I watched it again. I slowed it down. I zoomed in. I froze the action. By this time Miles had returned and I called him over.

"Look at this," I said.

"Honey, no offense, but I've seen it."

"No, seriously, look." He bent to look over my shoulder, and I made him watch the last few frames of the video in slow motion and then froze it at the point at which Flame was almost to the finish line and Neil, half turned from the camera, extended two fingers down toward the ground. "I saw him make that same hand signal this afternoon, and Flame came right to heel. Ginny said all his dogs are trained to hand signals, that's how he can send them around the course without saying a word—as long as they can see him, of course. So when he fell, he started calling the commands—but he never told her to take the last two jumps. She was trying to do that on her own, until she made the turn at the last jump and he was suddenly in her line of sight again. Then, here…" I pointed. "He called her back with a hand signal no one could hear." I frowned. "That must be what Marcie meant when she said, 'I saw what you did.' And why she was so mad—apparently they have some kind of contract about the dogs, and she was claiming he was in violation. But why in the world would he do that? Flame is partly his dog, too."

"Easy," Miles said, straightening. "Fifty

thousand dollars."

I stared at him. "What?"

"Didn't you just say he co-owns that dog? That means he has to split any winnings on it fifty-fifty."

I scowled, not because his theory didn't make sense, but because it did.

"Their contract probably calls for due diligence," Miles added, "so he couldn't refuse to handle the dog and do his best to win—or at least make it look that way."

"But if he doesn't go to the Standard Cup, he doesn't get the money, either," I pointed out.

"You'd be surprised what a man will do to screw his ex out of alimony," replied the man who'd been divorced three times.

Apparently I couldn't keep the suspicion out of my eyes because he held up a quick hand in self-defense. "Present company excepted, of course."

Then he said, "Listen, hon, as much as I'm enjoying it, I'm going to have to cut out on this shindig a little early. I'm meeting one of my architects back on Edisto at four and it's an hour drive. Do you need any help packing up this stuff before I go?"

I couldn't hide my disappointment. "I have another run today!"

"I know, and I can't wait to hear about it. I know you'll kick butt."

I stood and watched him fold up his camp chair and gather his cap and sunglasses. Cisco, sensing something interesting was about to happen, lifted his head from his bone alertly. "So is that why you came here?" I accused skeptically. "To meet with your architect?"

"Of course not. I came to be with you. And," he confessed because he was, for the most part, an exasperatingly honest man, "to meet with my architect."

Miles and I have a fairly casual relationship. Monogamous, but casual in the sense that I don't keep tabs on him and he doesn't keep tabs on me. His home base is Atlanta; mine is North Carolina. He flies to Dubai for the weekend and I pack up the SUV for a three-day dog show and neither of us feels the need to inform the other of our plans unless it comes up in conversation. I like it that way. I certainly didn't expect him to check with me before he went on a business trip. Still…

"What's in Edisto anyway?"

"A beachfront condo project."

"Oh, for Pete's sake, Miles! When are you ever going to stop pillaging the environment and improving on nature with a bulldozer?" And even though I wasn't really surprised, I was a little disappointed to learn he hadn't made the trip just to support me at the agility trial. That probably made my tone grumpier than it should have been.

"I'm not pillaging," he replied mildly, glancing one last time at the screen of his phone. "In fact, this is an award-winning eco-friendly design."

"Oh, I'm sure the sea turtles appreciate that. Not to mention all the residents who can't wait to see their beach turned into a tourist trap."

"Hate to tell you, hon, but it already is. There are more condos on that beach than seashells, and mine is the only one that's moving toward a negative environmental impact."

I really didn't enjoy being outmaneuvered in my own area of expertise. I glared at him. "There is such a thing as 'greenwashing,' you know."

"I sure do. There's a ton of federal money available for it. "

"Oh, for heaven's sake, Miles." Exasperation was exactly what I felt for him at that moment. "Is work the only thing you know how to do? Don't you ever play?"

"Absolutely." He took out his keys and snagged a mini bag of cheese puffs from my snack collection, presumably for the drive. "Eighteen holes every Tuesday and Thursday, weather permitting."

"Will you be back tonight?"

"Probably not," he admitted. "It depends on how long the meeting runs. Enjoy dinner with your friends. It's on me."

"You'd better believe it," I muttered, hiding my disappointment with a scowl. Now I knew why he'd been so quick to suggest I have dinner with Aggie. But if I'd known he wasn't going to be there, I *really* would have preferred room service.

He came forward and kissed me, gently but thoroughly, then tilted my chin with his index finger and smiled into my eyes. "See you tomorrow, okay?"

By now you're probably wondering just what I see in Miles, anyway. Perhaps I've failed to mention his eyes. And his smile. And there's that whole kissing thing.

I was just about to forgive him and send him on his way when there was a commotion outside. Cisco stood up, ears forward, and barked. I glanced toward the door just as a black-and-white blur streaked by, and I heard the most dreaded words of any dog show: *"Loose dog!"*

The echo hadn't even faded before my own dog scrambled past me, barking gleefully, and sailed over the gate.

CHAPTER SIX

Twenty-one hours, thirty-two minutes before the shooting

The only thing faster than a border collie at an agility trial is a runaway border collie at an agility trial. Cisco on a mission might run a close second. That being said, the entire thing was over in a matter of seconds.

I bolted to the gate and stumbled through, shouting for Cisco, just in time to see my champion careening after the border collie, his ears slicked back and his golden tail whirling, a grin of pure delight on his face. They raced down the corridor that divided the livestock barn and out into the sunshine, a chorus of barking following them. A dozen curious heads appeared from within the stalls as the two burst from the barn and made a beeline toward the open field. Along the way, others took up the chorus, "Loose dog! Loose dog!"

As everyone knows, the worst thing you can do when your dog is running away is to chase him. A dog being chased only runs faster, delighted with the opportunity to prove once again to all concerned that nothing on two legs will ever match the speed of a canine on four. Nonetheless, when your dog is headed toward the horizon at the speed of light, it's almost impossible *not* to run after him, so run is what I did.

I reached the outside of the barn just as Miles called, "Raine, catch!"

I spun around and snatched the bag of cheese puffs he tossed from the air. I called, "Cisco, here!" and snapped open the bag in the same moment.

Cisco had to be fifty yards away, but, like most dogs, he can hear the opening of a treat bag from the other side of the continent. He stopped, turned, pricked his ears, and raced back to me, the little border collie tearing along beside him. They were in full-out play mode now and were not about to break up the team.

From out of the corner of my eye I saw someone jogging in my direction and I heard her call out, but I was entirely too focused on my dog to pay much attention. Cisco galloped toward me, his eyes on the bag of cheese puffs and the border-collie zigzagging at his side, when I heard a woman call, "Bryte, come!" The border collie veered off and Cisco's head turned in her direction. I called, "Cisco, no!" and he swung back. The two dogs collided, rolled in the dust, and bounced up again just as the woman plowed into the fray, moving too fast to stop. She went down in a tangle of arms and legs and paws and tails.

You might think the proper thing to do in a situation like that would be to rush to help the fallen, but if I had done that I would have lost both dogs again. So I mustered my most commanding voice, said again, "Cisco, *here*," and plunged my hand into the bag of cheese puffs. Both dogs skidded to a stop in front of me.

"Hold on to her!" cried the woman, stumbling to her feet.

I slipped the leash that I keep perpetually draped around my shoulders over Cisco's neck and plied both dogs with cheese treats and praise while the woman hurried toward us. I glanced at her long enough to inquire, "Are you okay?" and I saw it was Neil Kellog's girlfriend, Marcie.

Her white shorts were covered in dust and dog

slobber and her tee shirt was ripped from collar to hem, apparently the victim of a careless dog claw. She held the remnants closed with one hand, barely covering her satiny bra, as she grasped Bryte's ruff with the other.

"Thank God you caught her," she said, gasping. "This is Neil's dog. I was putting her back in her crate when she took off. She never would listen to me. He'd kill me if anything happened to her."

This was a far different woman than the one I'd seen arguing with Neil earlier, and the fact that she seemed inclined to overlook Cisco's part in the fiasco—as well as her own bleeding knee—made me more disposed to like her than I had been earlier. I noticed Bryte wasn't wearing a collar, and I said, "Hold on. I've got a spare leash."

I took Cisco back to our stall and zipped him securely inside his crate. "This is starting to look more like the roller derby than a dog show," observed Miles as I dug through my bag for a first aid kit and spare leash.

"I just hope she doesn't realize it was Cisco who tripped her," I muttered in reply. I grabbed my spare sweatshirt from the bag and ran back out to Marcie.

"Here," I said, offering her the sweatshirt.

"Yours is kind of…" I made a fluttering gesture across my chest to indicate the scraps of her tee shirt that remained.

She looked up from dropping the loop leash over Bryte's neck and seemed surprised at the extent of the damage as she glanced down at her clothes. "Oh," she said, once again pulling the pieces together with one hand. She accepted the sweatshirt and transferred Bryte's leash to me. "That's nice of you…"

"Raine," I supplied. "Raine Stockton."

"I'm Marcie Wilbanks. Thanks," she added, "for catching Bryte. And for this." She managed a quick, if weak, smile as she nodded toward the sweatshirt.

"I brought these too." I held out a package of antiseptic wipes. "You should probably take care of that knee."

She turned away to pull on the sweatshirt and clean her injured knee, and I took advantage of the moment to slip my phone out of my pocket and snap a photo of myself with Bryte. I tapped out the caption, "Here I am with National Champion Bryte!" and sent it on to Facebook. Melanie would get a kick out of that.

"What ▓▓ ▓▓▓ are you doing with my dog?"

I barely had time to get to my feet and stuff my phone back into my pocket before Neil Kellog snatched Bryte's leash from my hand with such abruptness that the dog's two front feet left the ground as he jerked her to his side. "Hey!" I objected. "There's no need for that!"

"Calm down, Neil." Marcie came forward quickly. "She's okay. She got out of her crate and went for a run, but this girl caught her. You should be thanking her—"

Neil turned on her. His face was red and his eyes were snapping furiously. "So this is your game now? Stealing my dog? Do you really want to play by those rules, Marcie? Do you?"

"Are you crazy? Nobody tried to steal your dog!"

"Yeah, I'm crazy all right! Crazy for thinking I could trust you with her. The minute my back was turned—"

"Oh, for ~~heaven~~'s sake, Neil, it was an accident! If you hadn't trained her with that cockeyed method of yours, she would've come when I called her and—"

"I'll show you *accidents*, Marcie." He took a step toward her that couldn't be construed as anything but threatening. I could see the veins on the side of his neck bulging. "If you ever touch my dog again, you can look forward to an accident that will take you weeks to get over."

I said, trying to sound reasonable, "Listen, any dog can get loose. The important thing is—"

He turned on me. The color of his face and the fire in his eyes actually made me shrink back. "Who ~~the hell~~ are you?" He was in my face, practically roaring at me. I threw up an instinctive hand in self-defense. "You need to stay out of this if you know what's good for you!"

"~~For the love of Pete,~~ will you lower your voice?" Marcie caught his arm and he flung her away. She stumbled back.

"Everything okay here?" A hand fell lightly upon my shoulder, the touch casual, the gesture unmistakably protective. And though Miles's tone was mild, I didn't have to turn to look at him to feel the steel in his eyes. I'd seen that look before, and I could see it now in the way that Neil, subduing the blaze of anger in his face, looked away and scowled. I could see it in the breath of relief that passed through Marcie's parted lips. And I could hear it in Neil's tightly muttered, "I'm taking Bryte home." He turned on his heel and strode away with Bryte prancing to keep up.

Alarm flashed in Marcie's face. "You can't do that!" She ran after him. "Stop right there! That's not our agreement!"

I blew out a long, slow breath and turned to look at Miles. I felt as though I should apologize on behalf of the AKC—he was, after all, a guest of the sport—but I honestly didn't know what to say. He said it for me.

"Roller derby," he repeated. He squeezed my shoulder and added, "Do me a favor and stay out of that guy's way, okay? I don't like the way his eyes were spinning around in his head."

I shrugged uneasily. "Some people get a little carried away when it comes to their dogs."

He pretended surprise. "You don't say." Then he winked and tugged my ponytail. "Okay, I'm outta here. Text me your score."

"Time," I corrected him. "In agility, it's time."

"Right."

I couldn't help smiling as I tiptoed to brush a kiss across his lips. "Thanks for coming, Miles," I said, because, as my mother always said, you should never fail to reward the effort. "That was nice of you. It showed real character."

"Hey, I'm all about character." His eyes danced with amusement and he cupped my neck lightly as he turned to go. "Run fast." His phone rang and he took it out, glancing at the screen. "Love you, babe," he said, and blew me a kiss just before he punched a button and said into the phone, "Yeah, I'm on my way."

I just stood there in silent astonishment, watching him walk away.

CHAPTER SEVEN

Nineteen hours before the shooting

For the longest time after Miles left, I continued to stare after him, thinking, *Oh no, he didn't*. He did not just use the L word for the first time twenty minutes before I had to psych myself up for a run and he did not just walk away without giving me a chance to say anything in return. Was he kidding me? Seriously?

On the other hand, what would I have said? Our relationship was casual. I liked it that way. What was he thinking?

That was just it. He wasn't thinking. Men rarely are. FALSE!

By the time I finished walking Cisco and took him over the warm-up jump a couple of times, I'd decided I was making much ado about nothing. Miles hadn't meant anything. He probably even didn't remember saying it. Men were such idiots.

87

As I walked the jumpers-with-weaves course with the rest of my group, trying to memorize a complicated S-turn and wondering if I could do a blind cross coming into the second set of weave poles, I started to wonder what kind of man could just toss off "I love yous" so easily. How did you even get into that habit? On the other hand, wasn't it better to be too free with the words than afraid to say them at all? Or was it?

Standing in line waiting our turn, I came to the conclusion that I was the one who was the idiot and really, I needed to just let it go. Like my mother always said, the only thing more futile than trying to figure out why men did the things they did was trying to figure out what they were thinking when they did them. So I decided to just forget about it.

Unfortunately, in the process, I also forgot the S-turn and the blind cross, sent Cisco into the weave poles backwards, and called him off a jump so abruptly that he knocked the bar. Worse, I'm pretty sure the judge heard me say a bad word in the heat of the moment. No one likes to lose, and the only thing that made it bearable was the way Cisco bounced across the finish line with his tail waving and a big grin on his face, as happy to have blown the course as he'd been to win only a few hours ago. I couldn't help but laugh. There's a saying in this game: no matter what happens, you still get to go home with the best dog in the world. And so I did.

Home, for the duration, was the Pembroke Host Inn five miles down the highway from the trial site. I packed up our gear before the event was over—no point waiting for a ribbon you have absolutely no chance of getting, right?—and was back at the hotel by four thirty. Dog people, like elite athletes and senior citizens, like to dine early and be in bed by ten, and I wanted to get to the dining room before the salad bar was reduced to scraps of lettuce and pickled beets.

The hotel was a dog lover's paradise. It was set far back from the highway and surrounded by a beautifully manicured green lawn in front, which, of course, meant nothing to seasoned dog travelers. We look for long winding paths and big open fields and well-marked dog walk areas with strategically placed trash cans. This one had all of those things, plus the added bonus of a central courtyard onto which all the sliding doors of the dog-friendly rooms opened, so the last doggie pit stop of the night could be made in your slippers and robe, if necessary. All designers of hotels should be so thoughtful. I wanted to nominate them for an award.

I stopped by the room just long enough to feed Cisco one of his specially prepared homemade energy meals from the mini refrigerator—oatmeal, chicken livers, eggs, milk solids, and mixed vegetables—and check my phone messages. Miles had texted twice: *How did you do?* and *Running late. Call you after dinner.* Melanie had tweeted two pictures of the Smithsonian that made me smile reminiscently and texted, *Go, Cisco! My blue ribbon guy!* A later text added, *Touring the White House tomorrow. Boooring. Rather see you guys win another ribbon.*

I texted back, *Tell the Prez I said hi.* Then, *P.S. Maybe you'll get to see the First Dog!*

By this time Cisco had licked his bowl clean and lapped up half a bowl of water, so I snapped on his expandable leash, tucked the room key and a couple of pick-up bags in my pocket, and took him out for his evening walk. Just as in the Old West a cowboy always took care of his horse first, in the dog world we make sure our dogs are well fed and comfortable before we take care of ourselves. It's only right.

We went through the hallway door, which led

to the parking lot and the big open field beyond, and I noticed a couple of other dog walkers had the same idea. I saw Aggie with Gunny at the edge of the field and waved. She waved back, and we started toward them at a leisurely pace, Cisco in an ecstasy of sniffing the tracks of other dogs. When we reached the edge of the parking lot, I gave him a few extra feet on his expandable leash, and he hurried ahead of me.

I heard a car door slam behind me and glanced around to make certain no other dogs were heading toward us. Marcie was leaning against her blue minivan with one arm wrapped around her chest and the other hand covering her mouth, head bowed, clearly upset. I actually turned to start toward her, and then the driver's side door opened and a man came around the van. I thought it was Neil until I saw the tender way he took Marcie in his arms to comfort her, and then I realized he was a much bigger man than Neil and quite a bit blonder. He said something in a low tone, and in a moment she nodded and smiled up at him. He kissed her.

"Well, well," I murmured to myself. But that wasn't the most surprising thing I saw. When they went around to the back of the van and opened it, two dogs got out—Bryte and Flame. And I distinctly remembered Neil saying he was taking Bryte home.

The man slung the strap of a day bag over his shoulder and they started toward the dog walk area on the other side of the building. It was at that moment that Cisco reached the end of his leash and looked back at me inquiringly. I called him to my side because I didn't want there to be any misunderstanding about who was walking whom, then gave him the full twenty feet of expandable leash in which to explore, and we made our way across the field.

I spent a few minutes chatting with Aggie, and just as we were heading back to the hotel, Cisco saw Brinkley and his mom—whose name I finally discovered was Sarah—coming across the field. Of course there was no way I could take Cisco inside then, so we spent another ten or fifteen minutes letting the three goldens sniff and play-bow and romp with each other as much as their leashes would allow. We made arrangements to meet for dinner in half an hour and started back toward our rooms. The other two women went west and I went east, so I was probably the only one who noticed Marcie and her boyfriend walking the dogs across the field a few hundred feet away. I waved to her, and I know she saw me, but her boyfriend caught her arm quickly and they deliberately turned and went the other way. Odd, but I supposed they wanted privacy. Besides, just then I got another text from Miles and was reminded that I had enough to deal with in my own personal life without borrowing other peoples' problems.

CHAPTER EIGHT

*Eighteen hours, forty minutes before the
shooting*

Twice a week, Buck and Wyn met for
dinner at a steak house on the highway
midway between their two homes. The
food was good, and it was usually so late by the
time they got there that the family hour was over
and the place was relatively quiet. The restaurant
was open until midnight, so they could relax in a
booth over dessert and coffee for an hour or two
and unwind from the day.

Tonight, however, Buck was having a difficult
time leaving the day behind. And Wyn, who'd
always had one of the keenest detective minds he'd
ever known, was just as intrigued as he was over
the Berman case. She studied the file over a cup of
soft serve vanilla ice cream, her hair falling forward

to shadow her face as she absently licked the ice cream off the spoon.

"Bad dude," she observed, turning a page. "Three assaults, walked on every one. Forgery, fraud, possession… I can't believe he never did time before this."

"That's because he never came up before Judge Stockton before," Buck said. The red vinyl seat creaked as he leaned back against it, stretching out his legs, sipping his coffee. "Nothing ~~pissed off~~ *maddened* the judge more than a criminal who got off on a technicality. The thing is, he didn't blame the criminal—he blamed the law. And if you were the arresting officer who screwed up and didn't get the right warrant or forgot to read a Spanish-speaking person his rights in Spanish, he not only made you wish you'd never walked into his courtroom, he'd make you wish you'd never been born before you walked out. He used to say we were the torchbearers, and he would always hold us to a higher standard, because if you couldn't count on the guys who fought on the side of right, then what were any of us here for?"

Wyn glanced up, smiling. "He sounds like a real old-fashioned hanging judge. Were you ever in his courtroom?"

Buck shook his head. "He retired before I joined the force. But he's the reason I went into law enforcement, and that's no lie. As a kid I spent just about as much time over at the Stockton place as I did at my own, and I guess he taught me pretty much everything I know about the justice system… and more than that, about <u>morality</u> and standing up for what was right. He was one of those legends, the kind you read about in books, like Daniel Webster or Justice Holmes… At least he seemed that way to me." He shrugged a little self-consciously. "A hanging judge? Not really. But he was a stickler for what was right."

Wyn nodded thoughtfully, scraping up the last spoonful of ice cream from her cup. "So why do you suppose he let this guy plead to second?"

"You got me."

Wyn finished her ice cream and turned the last page in the file. "Well, I don't see anything that would trigger an alarm bell here. Did you talk to his parole officer?"

Buck nodded grimly. "He was on a weekly schedule and hasn't checked in in two weeks."

"Uh-oh." Wynn put down her spoon. "That's not good."

"No. It's not." Buck took a sip of coffee.

"According to his parole officer, he was living with his brother and helping him out with his construction business. The brother hasn't heard from him in a week."

"That he'll admit to."

"Right. He also hasn't seen one of the company pickup trucks in about that long."

"So we've got a recently released murderer—"

"Second degree," Buck reminded her.

"Right, second degree murderer that the trial judge was worried about..."

"Nobody said 'worried,'" Buck corrected. "All Roe said was that the judge wanted to keep an eye on him."

She leveled a look on him. "Yeah, so maybe the guy was the judge's long lost illegitimate son or the innocent victim of a frame and he wanted to make sure prison wasn't too hard on him. The judge was worried about Berman getting out. He served all but five years of his sentence, which means he was no angel in prison. He hasn't checked in with his parole officer in two weeks and he seems to have gone on the road. So what we have to figure out is what Judge Stockton was worried about. Who did he think this guy would go after when he got out?"

"Yeah." Buck blew out a breath. "That's all

we've got to figure out."

Wyn said casually, "Did you talk to Raine?"

The two of them had come to an understanding early in their relationship that there was no way to keep Raine's name from coming up now and again. Buck had known her all his life and had been married to her most of it. Wyn had been friends with Raine before... well, before. All of their lives were entwined, and they always would be. Still, it was awkward. And Buck couldn't prevent an automatic shifting of his gaze when he heard her name. He didn't like it when his worlds collided, or even brushed up against one another. He never knew how to react.

"No," he replied, "the judge never discussed his cases with the family. Besides, that was twenty years ago. She was just a kid. What would she know? Maude might remember something though," he added. "Maybe I'll give her a call tomorrow."

Wyn reached across the table and snagged his pinky finger with her own. "You know," she reminded him gently, "it *was* twenty years ago. The person who put in the notification request is dead. I wonder if..."

She let the sentence trail off and started to look

away, but Buck held her gaze. "If I'm making a bigger deal out of this than it needs to be. And if maybe the reason I'm doing it is because of Raine?"

Wyn pulled her hand away. "Okay," she said quietly. "Maybe."

He was silent for a moment, his eyes clear and thoughtful. "I've thought about that. If it had been anybody besides Judge Stockton, I might've let it go. Maybe I should let it go."

Wyn said, "But?"

He took another sip of coffee, glanced at his cup, and set it on the table. "But," he said simply, "my gut tells me that would be a big mistake."

She looked at him for a time, saying nothing. Then she nodded once, slowly, and opened the file again. "Okay," she said. "So let's start at the beginning. 9:15 p.m., some guy bearing a striking resemblance to Berman robs the Cash-n-Carry on Highway 11 of two thousand sixty-four dollars, in the process shooting one Gerald Sailor, night clerk, who later died of his injuries. Witnesses claimed that in the act of making his escape, the perpetrator scraped his vehicle—a reddish-brown Chevy pickup truck—against the pylon next to the pumps. No security tape, huh?"

Buck shook his head. "It was just a mom-and-pop place. Still is, I guess, but now they have cameras at the pumps and behind the register. Too many people driving off without paying, with the price of gas so high. I get a call two or three times a week."

"Do you ever catch them?"

He shrugged. "If they're local. If not, I turn it over to the state patrol. But I guess the cameras are worth it for the small business owner now. Back then, not so much."

Wyn looked back down at the file. "Two hours later, Berman is stopped for DUI with two thousand fourteen dollars in cash in his glove box and a pistol matching the description of the one used in the robbery, along with a receipt from the Cash-n-Carry. Too bad the machine didn't time stamp it. His vehicle, a primer-painted 1989 Chevy pickup, showed damage on the right front fender with streaks of green or blue paint." She glanced up at him. "So the only thing I'm wondering is why a guy would pay for twenty dollars worth of gas, save the receipt, and then rob the cash register at gunpoint."

Buck frowned a little. "He was stoned. Who knows why they do the crazy things they do?" But the way he said it made her think he'd asked the same question.

"Who was his lawyer?"

"Court appointed. Don Kramer."

"Senior?"

"Junior. He would've been just starting out then. Naturally his old man would give him all the grunt work."

"Still, he must have done an interview."

Buck's lips tightened with a dry smile. "I need you back on the force."

"You just let me know when you make up your mind."

He reached for the folder with a small shake of his head. "Who am I kidding? I don't have time to go chasing down clues on a twenty-year-old crime. If there was anything there to see, Roe would've seen it. And I don't even know what I'm looking for."

"What you're looking for," Wyn reminded him simply, "is answers. Why Judge Stockton thought it was important to keep tabs on this guy for twenty years. Why he hasn't checked in with his parole officer in two weeks. What one thing has to do with the other."

"Which is probably nothing." Buck picked up the check. "Come on, let's get out of here. Long drive home."

"So," Wyn said as they stood at the register and waited for the clerk to swipe Buck's credit card, "what's the verdict?"

"About what?"

"You know about what. The one thing you haven't brought up all night."

He draped an arm around her shoulders as they walked out into the night. There were only a handful of cars in the parking lot, scattered like islands in a misty sea of mercury vapor lights. He said, "I talked to a guy in Asheville. He said they were going to have some openings in the police department next month."

She stopped walking and looked up at him. "You? Leave Hanover County?"

He said, "We talked about it. Maybe picking up and starting over some place new."

"Yeah, but... I thought you meant Fiji or Belize or some deserted Pacific island somewhere."

He laughed softly. "Yeah, well, baby steps. Your folks are up that way," he added, watching her, "and it would be good to work together again. That is, if you'd be interested..."

She bumped his arm gently with her shoulder. "Dope. I'm making twelve fifty an hour walking patrol around the hospital parking lot and living in a furnished studio apartment. Anything is a step up from that. But you've lived in Hansonville all your life. All your friends are there. Everybody knows you... You'd win the election, you know. Who would run against you? And more importantly, who would be better at the job?"

He replied simply, "I'll never be another Roe Bleckley. Maybe it's time I made my own place in the world."

He walked her to her car and waited while she unlocked the door. She had parked next to a streetlight, its base protected by a florescent yellow concrete bumper. Buck stared at the bumper, frowning a little. "Say, Wyn," he said, "you've been to the Cash-n-Carry, right?"

She glanced up at him as she slid into the driver's seat of her car, her face illuminated by the glow of the courtesy lights. "Sure. I stop there to fill up every time I leave your place."

"You remember what color the pylons are at the pumps?"

She was thoughtful for a minute. "I want to say yellow. Maybe that's just because most of them are. Safety yellow."

"Yeah," said Buck. "Most of them are. I wonder

if there was ever a time when they were painted green?"

"And if not," said Wyn, catching on immediately, "how did green paint get on Berman's truck?"

"And why didn't his lawyer follow up on that?"

Wyn smiled at him, recognizing the signs of a mind that had already left her, worrying at the knots of a tangled problem. "Let me know what you find out, okay?"

"Sure thing." He bent to kiss her, but his tone was absent, his caress routine. "You drive carefully now."

She laughed as she put the car in gear. "You, too, officer."

CHAPTER NINE

Nineteen hours before the shooting

Miles and I had had issues before over my habit of forgetting to turn on my phone and refusing to return texts when I was annoyed with him, and I had almost paid the price for it last winter when Cisco and I had been stranded in a blizzard and one lucky phone call had saved our lives. Since then he'd made me promise not to be out of touch, which, given that my lifestyle occasionally—and through no fault of my own—had put me in harm's way, was not an unreasonable request. Because I always keep my promises, even when I don't want to, I texted Miles as soon as I returned to the room. *On my way to dinner. Turning off phone.*

But before I could do that, the incoming message chime sounded. *Call me.*

Going to bed early. Long day.

How early?

Don't be needy.

The message came back with the speed of light: *Excuse me?*

I turned off my phone and pretended I didn't receive it.

I took a quick shower, changed into clean jeans and a tee shirt without a slogan on it (which is dress-up in the world of dogs) and patted makeup over the red-blue bruise across the bridge of my nose. I always travel with sheets from home to cover the hotel furniture, and I spread one of them over the small sofa in the sitting area and another across the bed, although Cisco really, really knew better than to get on the bed while I was away. I left him with a chew bone and the television tuned to Animal Planet, along with a promise to bring him back a treat from dinner. When dogs win blue ribbons, they get treats from dinner, no matter how many subsequent courses they blow. That's the rule.

The dining room smelled of fried chicken, broccoli, and steam tables and was already beginning to fill up, even though it wasn't quite six o'clock. Ginny and Aggie waved to me from a big booth, and I'd barely gotten settled before Sarah joined us.

"You won't believe what happened to me when I was taking Brinkley back in after our walk," she said. She was a red-haired woman with troubled brown eyes and a pale face that now seemed a little drawn. "I opened the outside door with my key card, you know, and it's always a little awkward trying to get the dog in because the door swings out."

We all murmured agreement. It was hard to manage the key card, the leash, and the heavy door without tripping or stepping on your dog's toes while trying to edge inside the door.

"Well, I was holding the door open with my shoulder and trying to get Brinkley untangled from his leash when I noticed this guy jogging toward me. He yelled at me to hold the door for him because he'd forgotten his key. Well, let me tell you, I lived in New York City for twelve years and you *never* fall for that line. I pulled Brinkley in as fast as I could and let the door slam, and when he reached it he actually pounded on the glass and cursed me like a sailor. So you girls be careful."

"Did you report it to the front desk?" I asked.

"I most certainly did. They even got someone from security down to take a description. That's why I was a little late."

"Maybe somebody really did forget his key," offered Ginny.

"Then he should have gone to the front desk and gotten another one," returned Aggie. "Sarah's right. You never let somebody into the building with your key."

Ginny rolled her eyes. "Well, I *know* that, Mother. I'm just saying, we don't always have to think the worst."

"And I'm just saying we all should walk our dogs in the courtyard tonight," said Sarah.

I raised my water glass. "I'll drink to that. I've had about all the drama I can take today."

At their questioning looks, I explained about how Bryte had gotten loose and Neil had made such a scene with Marcie. Aggie, of course, had heard about the incident but hadn't realized I'd been the one to catch Bryte.

"Doesn't surprise me a bit," she confided. "That Neil always had a temper, especially when it comes to his dogs. I wonder if she did it on purpose. Marcie, that is."

"Well, it seems to have worked out okay." I shrugged. "I saw Marcie with her boyfriend this afternoon, and they had both dogs."

Aggie looked at me alertly. "Her boyfriend?"

I groaned inwardly. I don't mind listening to gossip now and then, but I really *hate* to instigate it. I tried for a quick change of subject. "I think I saw prime rib on the buffet, and I promised Cisco I'd bring him back a treat. Does anyone want to check it out with me?"

Sarah took me up on it immediately. "Congratulations on your win!" she said as we slid out of the squeaky vinyl seat. "I can't believe Brinkley almost ruined your run. Next time I'll make sure we're on the other side of the fairgrounds."

We laughed about the incident, and the conversation was successfully diverted to our individual runs as we all went to survey the buffet. We relived our triumphs and our training trials all through dinner and didn't think about Marcie again until she actually walked into the dining room.

She'd changed from her muddy shorts into jeans, but she still wore my sweatshirt. Her eyes looked puffy and her face looked shadowed, and I hesitated about waving to her, particularly considering the way she'd snubbed me earlier. Aggie, however, had no such reservations.

"Marcie," she called, waving her over. I remembered they were both members of the sponsoring agility club. "Come sit with us."

Marcie had a trapped expression on her face as she hesitated, glancing at the exit, but in the end she really had no choice but to come over and join us. I scooted over to make room for her.

"Hi," she said. She smiled, but her eyes looked haunted. The incident with Neil that afternoon must have upset her more than she'd indicated at the time. "I didn't know I'd see you here, or I would've returned your sweatshirt."

"Don't worry about it," I assured her. "I'll be at the site tomorrow."

"We had the buffet," Ginny said. "It was pretty good. The fish was actually crispy."

"I'm not staying," Marcie said. "I just came in to see if I could get some yogurt for Flame. Her stomach's a little upset."

We all made sympathetic noises. There is nothing worse than staying at a hotel with a sick dog.

"I hope she didn't pick up something contagious," Sarah said, and Marcie shook her head.

"No, Bryte's fine. Flame has always been

sensitive. I'm sure it's nothing."

"I'm glad Neil didn't take Bryte home after all," I said. "I'm looking forward to seeing her run tomorrow."

Marcie flashed a look to me that seemed, for the briefest of moments, laced with terror. Then she apparently remembered I'd actually been there when Neil took Bryte away, and she recovered herself with a quick, "Yes. Right." She cleared her throat and added, "Actually, of course, Neil only lives a few miles away now, so he probably would've brought her back for the trial tomorrow."

Aggie seized on this. "Really? I didn't know he'd moved."

Marcie nodded, running a hand over her throat in a nervous massaging motion. "He has an apartment in Pembroke. It doesn't allow dogs, even though he sneaks them in sometimes, so it's just temporary."

"I can't imagine Neil in a place that doesn't allow dogs," Ginny said.

"But you still have your beautiful place back in Derry, right?" Aggie persisted. "Gorgeous farm," she explained to the rest of us. "A huge training building, regulation agility course, fenced and cross-fenced... We have club picnics there sometimes."

Sarah said, "I'm confused. I thought Neil owned both the dogs. Are you just boarding them?"

"No." Marcie's tone was bitter. "They're my dogs. We co-own Flame, Shine, and Thunder, but he talked me into signing over Bryte to him when she was six months old. People do stupid things when they're in love, but that was by far the stupidest one I've ever done." I could see her jaw tighten from where I sat. "They live with me, though. He's not allowed to take them off the property except for shows. That's our agreement. I don't trust him out of my sight with those dogs. You wouldn't either."

The curiosity practically sparked across the table, but only Aggie had the courage—or the tactlessness—to ask what we were all thinking. "How come?" she inquired. She leaned in close across the table, her huge bosoms nudging her tea glass, her tone confidential and inviting. "You know, everybody's heard he amps his dogs up with meds. Somebody said he uses shock collars."

Marcie stiffened. "That's ridiculous. I would never allow anyone to abuse my dogs."

Everyone at the table could feel the situation

deteriorating, but Aggie soldiered gamely on. "Well, of course not, but you know there are some people who would do anything to win. And there's a lot at stake at this level."

The sound of the silence from Marcie was like ice cracking. I think everyone at the table, with the exception of the two women in the end seats, wanted to slide under it, myself included. And then Ginny, God bless her, turned to me and said brightly, "Say, Raine, I was meaning to ask you, where's that handsome fellow of yours tonight?"

I blinked at the non sequitur, then smiled. "Paying for dinner, as a matter of fact," I replied cheerily. "Let's order dessert."

*   *   *

I fed Cisco the leftover tidbits of prime rib that I sneaked out of the dining room wrapped in a napkin in my purse, and even though I made him do a trick for each one, he looked at me with such an expression of worshipful adoration on his face that I laughed out loud with delight and let him gobble the last few bits directly from the palm of my hand, no tricks required. Seriously, there's nothing better in this world than the unconditional love of a dog. Nothing.

The room telephone was ringing when I came back from washing my hands, and I knew I had to answer it.

"You forgot to turn on your phone," Miles said.

"I didn't forget." I sat down on the bed and kicked off my shoes.

"Uh-oh. Bad day after I left?"

"No. What makes you say that?" I knew my voice was stiff, but I couldn't help it.

He paused. "Are you mad at me about something?"

"What makes you say that?"

He said slowly, "Okay." Then, "I have a breakfast meeting in the morning, so I think I'll stay over."

I was both relieved and disappointed. "Okay. Good. That's a good idea."

There was another pause. "So how did you do in your last event?"

"We lost."

"Ah, well. Win some, lose some, right?"

"Jumpers-with-weaves," I said sourly, remembering it was all his fault we'd lost. "That's our best thing. We lost."

"Everybody has an off day."

"I guess. Whatever." But it *was* our best thing.

"Do you want to talk about it?"

"No. It's fine. It's just a game."

"Okay." A note of impatience, or perhaps frustration, crept into his voice. "What's wrong?"

"Nothing. It's just… I think we need to slow down," I blurted.

"What?"

"You. Me. I just think we might be moving too fast, that's all."

There was a beat, and the silence made me wince. When he spoke, his tone was guarded. "What brought this on?"

I licked my lips. I wished I'd never spoken. "It's just… you don't even know me. I don't know you. We hardly know each other. I don't think we should rush into anything, that's all."

"I hadn't planned to."

"Good." I swallowed. "That's good."

He said, "Is there something about me that you just discovered you don't know?"

I was taken aback. "Well, no. I was just thinking… Look, it's not something we have to talk about now…"

"Because we've been not knowing each other for over six months now, and this is the first I've heard you complain."

"I'm not complaining. It's just—"

"Are you mad because I left this afternoon?"

"No, of course not. Don't be silly." That was sincere, and he could tell it.

"Then it must be something I said."

I hesitated a split second too long. "Listen, Miles, let's not do this now, okay? I've got to be up at six and I'm really tired."

He said, "You know I'll figure it out, don't you?"

I was actually squirming. "Really, I've got to get some sleep. Good night, okay? And don't call back, please, because I'll be sleeping. You should sleep too. Good night." I hung up quickly and sat there for another half-minute or so, staring at the phone, willing it not to ring. It didn't.

Good.

I took Cisco out through the sliding doors to the courtyard for his last toilet break of the day, changed into my nightshirt, and was in bed by nine. I tossed and turned for ten or fifteen minutes, hearing every noise from the corridor outside, wishing the conversation had gone differently with Miles, but exhaustion and the gentle rhythm of Cisco's soft snore eventually lulled me into a dreamless sleep.

What seemed like only moments later, I was jerked awake by the shrilling of the bedside telephone. I rubbed my eyes open, staring at the red numbers of the digital clock. 11:45. Cisco stood beside the bed, tail wagging, wondering if it was morning. "Miles, you wouldn't dare," I muttered as the phone rang again. I fumbled for the receiver and snatched it off the hook.

"What?" I said ungraciously.

"Miss Stockton?"

I frowned. The voice on the other end was male, but it wasn't Miles. "That's right."

"This is the night manager. I'm afraid there's been a problem with your credit card. We need you to come to the front desk and clear it up."

I blinked, looking again at the clock. "Now?"

"Yes, ma'am. You do have a dog in your room, don't you?"

"Of course I do. So does everyone else in this wing." I reached out to stroke the canine in question. "Do you know what time it is?"

"If you could just confirm your room number for me we might be able to straighten this out over the phone."

Alarm bells started to clang belatedly, and I sat

up straighter. "Who is this?"

The connection was broken.

Most people who travel on the dog show circuit are women, and most of them are traveling alone—except, of course, for their built-in canine bodyguards. Fortified with a mostly false sense of confidence born from the fact that their traveling companions were only a few thousand years ago tearing mastodons limb from limb and could, theoretically, still do the same to a human, they engage in what might otherwise be considered risky behaviors: walking in deserted areas after dark, loading and unloading their cars in the pre-dawn hours of the morning, fumbling over door keys with their arms full, and worst of all, leaving their room doors propped open with the latch while they run down to the ice machine or take their dogs out to pee "just for a minute." They are natural targets for savvy con artists or worse, and every year you hear one or two tragic stories. Fortunately, you also hear about all the latest scams, and this one, now that I was awake, was starting to feel a little obvious to me.

I dropped the receiver back into the cradle and fumbled in the dark until I found the switch for the bedside lamp. My throat felt a little dry as I pulled the phone closer and squinted at the numbers printed there. I dialed the front desk.

A pleasant woman's voice answered, and I asked to speak with the night manager.

"This is the night manager," she said.

My head started to hurt. I identified myself and said, "Some man just called here saying he was the night manager and that I needed to come to the front desk to straighten out a problem with my credit card. I think he was trying to lure me from my room."

I heard computer keys clacking in the background. "Please remain in your room," she replied quickly, either reading from a protocol manual or very well trained. "There is no problem with your credit card, Miss Stockton. Do you feel you are in any danger now?"

"No, but you have a lot of women traveling alone who are staying here this weekend. If there's some kind of weirdo playing pranks…"

"Yes, ma'am, I'll send a security guard to your room right away."

"No, don't do that," I groaned. "I don't want to talk to a security guard. It's almost midnight. All I want is to go back to sleep."

"Yes, ma'am, I understand. We'll take care of

the problem."

"But don't send anyone to my room. And don't call here, either. I'm sleeping."

"Yes, ma'am. I'm terribly sorry you were disturbed."

"It's okay. Just… good night."

I hung up and turned off the light, sinking back against the pillows. Eventually I heard Cisco circle his bed a few times and plop down with a sigh. But I lay awake for a long time, staring at the dark and listening to the faraway barking of a dog.

SATURDAY

CHAPTER TEN

Nine hours before the shooting

I awoke abruptly hours later, my heart pounding, aware that something had jarred me back to consciousness but having no idea what. The clock said 5:03. I lay very still, listening, and then I heard it again: the low, fierce rumble of Cisco's growl.

I sat up, and Cisco stood, stiff-legged, watching something intently on the other side of the room. I followed his gaze and my heart slammed against my chest. The silhouette of a man was clearly formed on the white drapery that covered my sliding glass door, backlit by the lights of the courtyard. Had I locked that door after letting Cisco out for the last time? Had I heard it click? I had, hadn't I? I couldn't remember.

Cisco's growl grew louder, and I heard fumbling at the door. Was that the click of the latch?

I whispered, "Cisco, here!"

He didn't need a second invitation. Cisco bounded onto the bed and I caught his collar, dragging him with me as I tumbled over the side of the bed and onto the floor, putting the bed between myself and the door just as it began to slide open. In the same motion, I grabbed the lamp from the bedside table, jerking the plug out of the wall. It was clumsy and unwieldy, but it had a heavy metal base and it was the best I could do.

I crouched down behind the bed with one arm around Cisco and the other hand gripping the lamp, trying not to breathe, straining to hear over the pounding of my heart the sound of the footsteps that moved stealthily toward me. Frantically I tried to remember where I'd put my phone before I went to bed. In the drawer? On the night table on the other side of the bed? In my purse? Was there any chance of reaching it before—

With absolutely no warning at all, Cisco suddenly bounded away from me, scrambling around the side of the bed toward the shadowy figure that approached. I cried out and lunged after him, swinging the lamp blindly. The intruder caught my arm in a grip of steel and the lamp crashed against the wall.

"For God's sake, Raine!"

I fell back, gasping, and Cisco flung himself in happy welcome upon the newcomer. Miles turned on the light. I blinked and squinted and for a moment didn't trust myself to speak. When I did, my voice sounded angry and hoarse.

"What are you doing here?" I demanded.

He frowned a little. "I paid for the room, remember?"

I remembered, a little irrelevantly, that, in fact, he had insisted on upgrading to a mini suite when he arrived, and this room wasn't even on my credit card. That seemed important somehow, but I was too upset at the moment to follow it through.

"You're also paying for a lamp," I told him shortly, picking up the dented lamp and setting it a little unsteadily on the table by the door. "What are you doing sneaking in here at this time of night anyway? Why didn't you use the front door?"

He gave Cisco's ears a final rub, and my faithful guard dog wandered over to check his food dish.

"Because the security bar is on the front door," he explained patiently, and of course it was. "I didn't want to wake you."

"Well, you did," I replied grumpily and stalked to the bathroom.

I returned wearing the same jeans and tee shirt I'd worn to dinner, face washed, hair pulled back, and a little calmer. At least my heart had stopped thundering and the raw taste of terror in my mouth had been improved by the taste of toothpaste. Miles had started the coffee pot at the minibar, and the warm smell of coffee filled the room. That softened my attitude toward him somewhat, but I wasn't ready to let him know. I sat down on the bed and pulled on my socks and running shoes.

"I'm sorry I scared you," he said.

There was no point in denying I'd been scared, even though I was embarrassed about it now. "What happened to your breakfast meeting?" I replied ungraciously without looking up.

"Rescheduled." He added mildly, "I figured it out."

I stood up and pulled my sweatshirt over my head. "What?"

Miles poured the coffee into two paper cups and handed me one. His eyes were easy and untroubled. "It's just something people say, Raine," he said. "I also love sunsets, sailing, and peach ice cream. It's just something you say."

I turned away, frowning, embarrassed, uncomfortable. I took a sip of coffee and it burned my tongue. "I have to walk Cisco," I muttered.

I plopped my baseball cap on my head, checked my pockets for pick-up bags, and reached for Cisco's leash. The minute he heard the clink of the swivel hook, Cisco bounced over to me and sat, his tail dusting the carpet with a happy swishing motion. I snapped on the leash and Miles opened the door for us.

A walk in the courtyard would have been sufficient this time of morning, but I wasn't thinking clearly. We went down the corridor and out into the parking lot, Miles accompanying us silently, sipping his coffee. A cool mist lay over everything, and the distant horizon was barely gray. The artificial yellow of the streetlights washed out the colors of the cars and Cisco's golden coat, covering everything in a flat, one-dimensional stain. In the distance the empty field spread out like a pool of spilled ink.

Cisco lifted his leg on a spindly bush at the edge of the field and then began an interested exploration of the scents left by all the creatures who'd passed by during the night. I lingered in the pool of light at the edge of the parking lot, not trusting my footing in the dark field. Since we were the only ones around this time of morning, I gave Cisco the full twenty feet of the leash to explore at leisure.

Miles said, "A couple of things you should know. First of all, I'm never getting married again."

I stifled a groan. "It's too early for this conversation, Miles."

"Better too early than too late. You said you didn't know me. Here's your chance."

I sighed, watching the plume of Cisco's tail fade into the gloom and low fog of early morning a few feet away. I tightened my thumb on the brake of the leash just to remind him I was there. "Okay," I said, resigned. "I'm glad you're never getting married again. You're terrible at it."

I could feel the weight of his gaze. "So nice to have that confirmed by an expert."

I sipped my coffee.

"I don't want any more children."

I said again, "Okay."

"And I never would've let you get close to my daughter if I didn't expect you to be in our lives for awhile. A long while. You really should've figured that one out for yourself."

I didn't know what to say. I really *should* have figured that out. I focused on the shape of Cisco's body at the end of the leash as though he were a life preserver and I were adrift in a dark sea. My throat felt a little tight, and I took another sip of coffee.

He bent a penetrating gaze on me. "I'm not going to be the rebound guy, Raine. You need to know that."

I swallowed hard. "You're not the rebound guy." It sounded a little muffled. "I wouldn't do that."

"Good. I didn't think so."

"Good."

"That means," he went on, "that I'm not going to let you get away with picking petty fights, and I'm not going to give up on you just because you keep trying to see if I will. Still, I wish you'd stop doing it. It's a waste of time."

One corner of my lips turned down dryly. "No more petty fights," I agreed. "We've got too many real things to fight about."

"True enough. One more thing you should know."

I glanced at him.

"My house is almost finished. Mel and I will be moving to Hansonville full time when she gets out of school. You'll be seeing a lot more of us."

Miles and I had met when he bought the mountain adjacent to my property and started scraping away the wilderness to make room for a ridiculous resort community complete with condos, golf courses, and an airstrip. Needless to say, our relationship had started out on a contentious note and I made no secret of the fact that we would always be on opposite sides of that particular issue. I knew he intended to build a house for himself on the property, but I'd never given much thought to the fact that one day he might actually move into it.

An odd mixture of delight and trepidation rippled through me. Part of me was thrilled, mostly because I did enjoy Melanie. Another part of me knew perfectly well there was a huge difference between the playful, mostly long-distance relationship Miles and I had sustained these past few months and the kind of relationship that would develop when we saw each other every day. When he became part of my world.

He went on. "So that's about it. If there's

anything else you need to know, I have a fairly comprehensive Wikipedia page."

"I know," I admitted. "I looked you up."

He chuckled and dropped a hand lightly upon the back of my neck, gently caressing. "So what is it you think I don't know about you that I need to know?"

I was uncomfortable, not at his closeness, which I enjoyed, but at his easy openness, which I could not reciprocate. The dawn was beginning to fade away the worst of the shadows, and Cisco tugged a little at the leash, so I followed him into the field. I said, "I don't like to talk about myself."

"So I've noticed."

"I think it's a Southern thing. Girls are taught to be modest."

He made a dry sound in the back of his throat and I glanced at him suspiciously. "Your modesty was the first thing I admired about you," he assured me with a perfectly straight face, and I scowled at him.

"Anyway, I really can't think of anything you need to know." I focused on Cisco and on picking my way across the stubbly ground. "I ▓▓▓ at this relationship thing. So do you. I'm a mess. You're a mess. We're a perfect team. I don't know what else to say."

"Let me help you out." He took a sip of his coffee. "You take a lot of chances—with everything except your heart."

I smothered a sniff of laughter. "That's pretty cliché." I really didn't like the way this conversation was going.

"My thoughts exactly." He went on. "You've never been really close to anyone outside the county you were born in, so I'd say you have a few trust issues. You seem to have a habit of marrying the same man over and over again. No offense to the sheriff, who I actually like, but you need to stop that."

I started to smile, but his next words wiped the smile away.

"You tend to get carried away by your passion for a cause, and last year that passion put you on the wrong side of an FBI investigation. It also put you in the arms of a known terrorist."

I stopped dead and stared at him in the dimness. He was watching me carefully. I said stiffly, "Andy and I had been friends since we were kids."

He said quietly, "Honey, I know about Andy Fontana. I know what happened and I know how it

ended. I'm not judging you. I just want you to
know I understand."

I didn't talk about Andy, not to Miles, not to
anyone. I tried not to even think about him, even
though sometimes I still woke in the night with my
cheeks wet with tears. There was no reason Miles
should *not* know about Andy, of course. The FBI
shootout had made all the papers and been local
headline news for weeks afterwards, and it
wouldn't take too much investigation to discover
that Andy and I had grown up together and had
shared an off-campus apartment in college. And
still I felt invaded. Perhaps not as invaded as I'd
felt last night when the creep called my room,
but...

I said suddenly, "He knew my name."

Miles looked understandably confused.
"What?"

I looked at him sharply in the dimness. "The
room is in your name. How would anyone know
how to reach me?"

"Do you mean besides on your cell phone?
They'd just ask the front desk to ring your room.
You're a registered guest. Your room number's on
the computer. We weren't trying to keep it a secret
that we were staying together, were we?"

"Weird," I murmured. I felt a chill run down my spine that was completely unrelated to the early morning damp. "But how would he know my name?"

"Who? Why do I get the feeling I'm no longer necessary to this conversation?"

"Sorry," I said. "It's probably nothing, just some random creep playing games."

"Okay, now you've got my attention." He looked at me intently in the grayish light, and there was no amusement in his tone now whatsoever. "What's going on?"

I started to explain about the phone call in the night, but the leash suddenly tightened in my hand, causing me to stagger and spill my coffee. "Cisco!"

Cisco glanced up around at me, then returned to sniffing and pawing at something in the grass. He could've uncovered almost anything, from a rotting animal carcass to a nest of fire ants, so I went quickly to investigate, calling as I did, "Leave it!"

Reluctantly, Cisco abandoned his treasure and sat, waiting for me to reach him. I'd like to say he was that prompt with all his commands, but "leave it" was one of those things we'd been working on since he was a puppy. It is essential in search-and-rescue work and has saved more than one dog's life. I was relieved to see that in this case Cisco's find didn't pose any immediate threat but was nothing but a piece of metal half-buried in a shallow mound of loose dirt and dried grass. I couldn't imagine why Cisco was even interested in it.

I picked it up and found that it was, in fact, an old lead pipe, damp with dew and mud. I looked at it curiously and let it drop again. Cisco took this as tacit permission to resume his pawing and sniffing, and I let him.

Miles said, "You were about to tell me about some random creep?"

"It's almost six o'clock," I said, glancing at my watch. "The dining room will be open by the time we get there. I'll tell you over breakfast." I tugged lightly on the leash and said, "Cisco, let's go."

But Cisco had other ideas. He suddenly looked up from nosing about the ground, swiveled his head toward the tree line on the opposite side of the field, and gave a single sharp bark. He took off at a lope before I could get my thumb on the brake of the leash, and I shouted, "Hey!"

I spilled more coffee as I spun around and

managed to bring Cisco to a halt, and then I saw what had gotten him so excited. A dog was galloping across the field toward us, and nothing good could come of that. I quickly passed my coffee cup to Miles and held on to Cisco's leash with both hands. As he had proven yesterday, a dog running loose was one of those things that simply wasn't within his power to resist.

No one else from the hotel had yet joined us in the dog-walking field, so I knew the animal had to be a stray. The way it was running at us with such determination made me uneasy, so I dug in my heels and pulled Cisco closer, trying to swing him away from the aggressor and back toward the parking lot. The last thing I needed was a dog fight. But Cisco panted with excitement, straining at the leash in his eagerness to greet the newcomer. The dog barked a greeting and was close enough now that I could see it was a border collie. And not just any border collie.

"Hey!" I exclaimed. "I think that's Flame!"

I was right. It was Flame, splashed with mud, covered in burrs, and trailing her leash. Her owner was nowhere in sight.

CHAPTER ELEVEN

Six hours, thirty minutes before the shooting

Miss Meg's Diner opened at six a.m. for breakfast, and on weekday mornings that was when everybody showed up: construction workers who had to be at the job site by seven, out-of-town workers who had a long commute, doctors and lawyers and insurance agents who opened their offices at eight but liked to see and be seen and didn't want to miss out on anything that was going on. On Saturday mornings, Miss Meg's diner was the place where the men of the town gathered between six and nine a.m. to solve the problems of the world, the country, the county, and their own home town. More than one mayor had been elected here before he was even nominated and county commissioners quietly relieved of office before the scandal broke.

There was a lot of loud talk about what the President should do, what was really wrong with this country, how to fix the economy once and for all, and who they really needed up on Capitol Hill. Meantime, deals were quietly made under the table and contracts illegally awarded and nobody said much about it because, after all, they were all friends here.

Hands went up and friendly greetings were called out when Buck came in just before seven, and he returned them in his usual easy fashion. He liked to hang out at the diner with the morning crowd when he got a chance; it was the best way to keep up with what was really going on around town. The trouble was that he rarely got a chance anymore, and today was no different. This was business.

Don Kramer Jr., Attorney At Law, was due in Saturday court at eight but had a vague memory of the Berman case and agreed to meet Buck for breakfast. Don Jr., as most people called him, bore such a striking resemblance to his father—right down to the horn-rimmed glasses, center-parted hair, and red bowtie—that it was almost impossible not to do a double take when they entered a room together. Even when they were separate, it was easy to mistake one for the other, and Buck often had to look carefully before he began discussing with one law partner a case that actually belonged to the other.

Don Jr. was sitting alone at a table for two, his briefcase on the floor beside him, the remnants of a breakfast that had consisted of half a grapefruit, whole-wheat toast, and oatmeal before him. "I glanced back over the case file while I was waiting," he said without preamble when Buck was seated, "to refresh my memory. What was it in particular that you wanted to know?"

Buck glanced around, hoping to catch the eye of a waitress with a coffee pot. "Well, for starters," Buck said, "Berman claimed he was innocent right up until the trial. What made him do an about-face and take a deal that ended up costing him more time than he would've done if he'd copped to all three of the charges he was arrested on, plus trafficking and hit and run?"

"He didn't have much choice, I'm afraid. Frankly, after we lost our strongest evidence I'm surprised the prosecutor even offered a deal. He could've been looking at the death penalty."

"What evidence?"

A harried waitress finally discovered Buck's

empty coffee mug and filled it with an absent smile before edging her way through the crowd of tables to attend another customer.

"The forensics report on his truck, the one he claimed was involved in a collision with another vehicle at the time of the shooting."

"I was wondering about that. What happened to it?"

"It disappeared."

Buck's brow knotted briefly as he sipped his coffee. "Did you subpoena the arresting officer in Georgia? He could have testified to the banged-up front fender, at least. It was in his initial report."

"I did." Don Jr. picked up a remaining corner of toast, buttered it neatly, and popped it into his mouth. He chewed and swallowed before finishing, "The judge disallowed testimony about the condition of the defendant's vehicle at the time of his arrest."

Now Buck was surprised. "Oh yeah? How come?"

The other man pursed his lips thoughtfully. "I believe it had something to do with weather conditions, unreliable evidence... It really didn't make much difference because without his pickup truck, or at least a forensics report, I didn't even know what I was looking for."

"You were looking," Buck informed him, "for yellow paint from the gas pump pylon that would definitively place him at the scene of the crime. Anything else would've corroborated his story, or at least given you reasonable doubt."

The blank look in the other man's eyes told Buck that, either that hadn't been part of the defense plan, or Don Jr. didn't remember the case as well as he had indicated.

"What about the other car?" Buck persisted. "What kind of attempt did you make to find it?"

"The usual. Repair shops, emergency rooms. But it was a bad winter and there were a lot of fender benders, if I recall. With no one willing to come forward about a hit and run, it was a dead end."

"Any description of the driver?"

"My notes say the defendant claimed a woman was driving with a man in the car, but that's about it. He didn't get a good look at the driver but swore up and down he'd recognize the passenger if he saw him again. He gave us a description of the man, but it was pretty general. There's no denying he was under the influence at the time. He would've hung himself on the stand, and if you ask me, the judge did him a favor."

"What do you mean, by letting him plead to second?"

Don Jr. took a final sip of his coffee, blotted his lips neatly, and shook his head. "He did more than that. The judge was the one who came up with the deal. He called Gill—Gilly Rogers, he's the one who prosecuted the case, may he rest in peace—Gill and me into his chambers and told us he wasn't allowing the arresting officer to testify about the truck and that I'd have to build my case on the testimony of the defendant, which, as we all knew, would be a waste of taxpayer's money. So he strongly suggested we reach an agreement and came up with one he'd approve. I guess you never got to work with the judge, but he used to do things like that, informally, always working to be fair to everybody. It sure did make the practice of law a lot easier back then, I'll tell you that." And he smiled mirthlessly. "Of course, our billable hours weren't nearly as high as they are now, either."

Buck sipped his coffee thoughtfully. "You said you didn't have Berman's truck for evidence. What happened to it?"

A look that was part rueful, part puzzled crossed Don Jr.'s face, and he gave a small shake of his head. "Talk about your crazy snafus. Somebody screwed up and forgot to tag it as evidence. It went up for auction before the trial, can you believe that?"

Buck raised an eyebrow. "I'm no lawyer, but that sounds like grounds for a mistrial to me."

"If we had gone to trial," agreed Don Jr., "I would've argued that being able to examine the truck was essential to our defense and I would've moved for a mistrial. But we never got that far. In fact, I didn't get the notice that the truck had been mistagged until a month or so after we'd struck the deal. You know how it is, trying to deal with those Georgia boys."

Buck gave a noncommittal shrug.

"I told the kid we wouldn't have a chance if we went to a jury, and that was the truth. Still, it took me right up to the wire to convince him to the take the plea. The ungrateful little punk kept going on about being framed, about the judge being out to get him, the cops stealing his truck…"

"Framed?" Buck said. "By who?"

Don Jr. shrugged. "He never got that specific. You know how it goes. I suspect the drugs had made him paranoid by then, among other things. Like I said, he was a cocky son of a gun, the kind that will spend his life blaming everyone but himself for his problems."

"So he took the deal, but he didn't like it, even though the judge was going out of his way to cut him some slack."

"He didn't see it that way. He said he was innocent." Don Jr. finished his coffee. "They all say they're innocent."

Buck asked, "Did he ever make any threats? Against you or anybody else involved with the case?"

The attorney seemed surprised. "Defendants rarely threaten their attorneys, Sheriff. It tends to weaken their chances in court." He thought for a moment. "No, I don't recall him threatening anyone in particular. Just the usual—he was being framed and somebody was going to pay, that kind of thing." He hesitated. "There was one thing. He asked to see me a couple of years after he was sent up. He said he had new evidence and wanted to reopen the case, but he wouldn't even tell me what it was unless I could make sure to move the trial to another county. I explained to him it didn't work that way, and I never heard from him again." He picked up his briefcase and stood. "I've got to get to the courthouse, Sheriff. Anything else?"

Buck shook his head absently. "No. Thanks, Don." Then he turned in his seat. "Say, Don."

The attorney looked back.

Buck said, "So you think if you'd gone to trial the jury would've brought back a murder one verdict, right?"

"No doubt about it. Local crime, local witnesses, local man dead... no doubt about it."

"Judge Stockton never was known to be soft on crime. Why do you suppose he pushed the deal?"

Don Jr. frowned a little. "I wondered about that myself at the time. The only thing I can figure is that he wanted the fellow off the streets and didn't want to go to trial."

Buck murmured, "I wonder why."

He shrugged. "I guess we'll never know, will we? Have a good day, Sheriff."

"Are you sure that's the right dog?" Miles said. "They all look the same to me."

I couldn't help slanting him an exasperated look. "Of course they do." But, in fact, he did have a point. If it hadn't been for the bright yellow flames embroidered on her leash, I wouldn't have recognized her either, and I'd still had to check the

ID tag on her collar to make certain. Not that it mattered. Whether it was an agility star or a house pet, a lost dog was top priority.

We'd waited for some time, listening for the sound of a frantic owner calling her dog, and then walked across the field, expecting Marcie to come running up at any moment. As the minutes went by and more people came out into the parking lot or crossed into the field to walk their dogs, I asked if anyone had seen Marcie, but no one had. Worse, no one knew what room she was in.

"She must have given up and gone back to her room," Miles said. "You should have the front desk call her."

If I'd lost Cisco in an open field next to a strange hotel far from home, I couldn't imagine just giving up and going back to my room. But it was getting late, and Cisco was competing in the first event, and I didn't know what else to do. "Yeah, okay," I said. "I guess so. They can at least leave a message for her if she's still out looking. Go on to breakfast. I'll meet you there."

"Do you want me to take Cisco to the room?"

Cisco was over the excitement of the new dog and was once again sniffing the grassy field, pausing to look up with pricked ears and happy eyes every time a car door slammed in the parking lot or another dog headed excitedly in our direction, pulling its owner behind. Flame, with the energy-conserving good sense of most border collies, lay down at my feet, waiting for what was going to happen next.

"No, I'll do it." I didn't want to give Cisco his breakfast until after he'd completed his first run, and Miles was notorious for sneaking him treats.

Miles nodded toward Flame. "What are you going to do with that one?"

"I don't know," I admitted. I clucked my tongue to both dogs, pulling Cisco into heel as we started back across the field toward the parking lot. "I guess I can take her with me to the trial and leave her in the car until Marcie gets there. It shouldn't be very long before she gets the message. I'll leave my cell phone number too."

I glanced at my watch and noticed to my dismay that it was almost seven. "Uh-oh," I said. "I don't think I have time for breakfast." I turned a beseeching look on Miles. "Would you do me a huge favor and grab a couple of pastries to go from the breakfast bar? And more coffee."

He gave me a look filled with forbearance. "I could be having eggs Benedict watching the sun

Donna Ball

rise over the ocean right now. So glad I cancelled my meeting."

"And bacon," I added, struggling to keep both dogs under a reasonable semblance of control. "For training treats. *Hey!*" I stopped dead and glared at the dogs, both of whom were straining and pulling at their leashes, eyes fixed upon the thick copse of woods that separated the field from the highway, having apparently caught the scent of a rabbit or a squirrel. "Cisco, watch me!"

Usually that tone of voice, which I admit shouldn't be used in crowded rooms or after midnight in public places, is enough to bring Cisco to a screeching halt and cause any other dog to snap to attention. In fact, Flame did whip her head around to look at me, her ears going down guiltily. Cisco fixed his gaze on the wood line and barked.

I gave the leash a quick sharp tug, just to get his attention, and finally he looked at me. "Cisco, heel!"

He looked at the trees and back at me with an expression that suggested he thought he might have misunderstood. Flame whined. I said firmly, "Wrong." And tugged the leash again. Reluctantly, Cisco came to heel.

"Maybe if you'd mentioned the bacon," Miles

murmured.

"I'll meet you at the car," I told him.

He went right and I went left, and as we crossed the parking lot toward the office, it took all my focus to keep the dogs' attention on me rather than the steady stream of canines headed out for their morning walk. As we came under the portico, I heard someone call hello, and I turned to see Aggie and Ginny with Gunny coming toward us. I waited for them.

Gunny was a gorgeous, high-stepping golden retriever who looked happy to greet the world this morning, and Cisco was equally as happy to greet him. This was where all of our Canine Good Citizen training came in handy, and we had plenty, since Cisco had failed the CGC test twice. Flame was no problem, tucking herself into a shy sit and half hiding behind my legs, but Cisco could barely contain himself, licking his lips and pounding his tail on the concrete, until Ginny and Gunny reached us and I gave him a quiet "say hello" command.

"He has such good manners!" exclaimed Ginny, and I managed not to roll my eyes as I watched the two dogs sniff and circle each other.

Aggie was only a few steps behind. "Who is

that you have there?"

"It's Flame," I told her. "We found her running loose this morning. Have either of you seen Marcie? She must be going crazy with worry."

Ginny shook her head and spoke softly to Flame as she reached to pet her. "Poor thing. She's a mess."

Aggie pursed her lips. "I know it's not nice to say, but don't you think it's a little strange, almost tit for tat, that after Neil's dog got loose yesterday it should be Flame who's running around loose this morning?"

Of course I did, but it *wasn't* nice to say. I said, "You don't happen to know what room she's in, do you?"

Aggie shook her head, and Ginny straightened up from petting Flame. "I wonder if that was Bryte we heard barking this morning. If she went out looking for Flame, she could have left Bryte in the room alone."

"It sounded like it was on the other side of the building, though," Aggie said. "I didn't hear it when we came out just now."

I said, "I'm just going to run in and ask the front desk to ring her room. Do you mind holding Flame for me?" I passed the leash to Aggie, and

Gunny lost interest in Cisco and began sniffing Flame. Flame, who'd had a hard morning, lifted a corner of her lip in warning. Aggie took a step backward, nudging Flame out of range, and Ginny did the same with Gunny. I love being around professional dog people. "I'll just be a minute," I said. "Cisco, with me."

Cisco got his share of oohs and ahhs from the few non-dog people who were in the lobby and indulgent smiles from the other competitors who were walking through with their cups of coffee on the way to the trial site. He was awfully cute, I had to admit, now that he was out of the path of distraction and had nothing to think about but walking in perfect heel position with his head held high, his coat shimmering, and a winning grin on his face. Somebody said, "He looks just like that dog in the television commercial!" and I wanted to reply, "Which one?" Because as the whole of Madison Avenue knows, if you want to sell anything from a car to underwear, all you have to do is get a good shot of a golden retriever in the ad.

The only person who didn't look happy to see us was the desk clerk, and I remembered too late that the hotel had a policy about dogs in the lobby. However, her disapproving scowl immediately evaporated when I introduced myself and she typed in my room number.

"Oh, Miss Stockton, I hope everything is okay this morning," she said. "The night manager left a message that you were not to be disturbed, but she wanted you to know that the hotel is thoroughly investigating your complaint, and the head of security will be happy to sit down and talk with you whenever you wish."

I wasn't entirely sure what "thoroughly investigating my complaint" consisted of, but I appreciated the gesture. And since all's well that ends well, I said, "I may take you up on that later, but right now I was hoping you could ring a guest's room for me. She's lost her dog and I want her to know I've found it. Her name is Marcie Wilbanks."

Once again the desk clerk tapped a rapid series of keys. "I'll be happy to do that, Miss Stockton, but we've already left several messages. We had some complaints about her dog barking during the night. I don't think she's in her room."

Nonetheless, she picked up the receiver, dialed the number, and waited politely while it rang. Eventually, she gave me an apologetic shrug and hung up. "If you'd like to leave a message, I'll be sure she gets it."

She gave me a pad and paper, and I wrote my name, room number, and cell phone on it, along with a brief message telling her I was taking Flame with me to the trial site and she could pick her up at our campsite in the livestock barn. I wished it had turned out differently, though. I didn't like to be responsible for someone else's dog when I already had my hands full with Cisco, especially considering the way Neil acted yesterday. He was just as likely to accuse me of stealing the dog as to thank me for rescuing her.

When I left the office and didn't find Ginny and Aggie waiting outside with Flame, I was at first relieved. Marcie must have returned, after all, and the runaway dog was no longer my problem. I should've known better, particularly when the first thing Cisco did upon leaving the building was swivel his head toward the left and stop so abruptly I almost tripped over him. When I looked around I saw several people with dogs were gathered at the edge of the parking lot. Aggie and Ginny were among them. Flame was not.

"I was going to put her in the back of our van," Aggie said with a shake of her head, "while we loaded the cooler and crate, and she slipped her collar. She took off toward the woods like a crazy thing."

Sarah was there with Brinkley. "At least she's not running through the brush with a lead on. It's a wonder she didn't choke herself the first time."

"Someone should call Neil," someone else said. "After all, it's his dog. Partly, anyway. Does anyone have his number?"

"The trial secretary might," said Ginny. "She's already at the site, though, setting up." She glanced at her mother. "We should get going, too."

And even as I started to quickly agree that yes, someone should definitely call Neil—that was exactly what someone should do, because Cisco and I were entered in the first event of the morning and we had to leave within the next fifteen minutes if we were to have any chance of warming up before the run—I felt my heart sink to my toes. Brinkley stood less than five feet from Cisco, yet Cisco was completely ignoring him. Cisco sniffed the ground, and then the air, his tail up, his expression intense, his whole body leaning toward the wood line. He was working, and not even Brinkley could tempt him away from his quarry.

Resignedly, I held out my hand for Flame's leash. "I think Cisco can track her. We can try, anyway. If we find her I'll bring her with me to the trial."

Aggie and I exchanged cell phone numbers so that we could keep in touch about Marcie, and she promised to call me if she was able to find out how to reach Neil. I looped the leash around my neck and released the brake on Cisco's expandable leash. I brushed the ground with my fingers. "Cisco, track."

The ground was still damp enough to hold a strong scent and Cisco took off eagerly. I had to trot to keep up for the first few dozen yards, which was okay because that would probably be the only warm-up either of us would have that day, assuming we even made it in time for our first run. As we reached the part of the field where other dogs had crossed, however, Cisco slowed down, taking his time to distinguish between older and more recent scent trails. I pulled out my phone and dialed Miles.

"You're late," he answered.

"Sorry." I was still breathing hard from the run. "A slight delay."

"Are you okay? You sound winded."

"I am. The dog got away again."

"Then you won't mind if I eat your bear claw."

Donna Ball

"Miles," I said, "you don't have to stay. You should go back to your meeting. My schedule is all screwed up anyway and there's no point in you coming out to the fairgrounds again today. You should go do your thing and I'll see you tonight."

"Are you trying to get rid of me?"

"Kind of. I feel bad about making you drive back this morning."

We'd reached the far end of the field and Cisco, twenty feet ahead, plowed into the brush. Shielding my face against flapping branches with my arm, I gamely followed him.

"You didn't make me do anything. But that does remind me. What's the story with the random creep playing games?"

"Hold on," I said.

"No chance. I'm not going anywhere until…"

I took the phone away from my ear and concentrated on keeping my balance as I struggled after Cisco through the piney woods and undergrowth. I thought I heard a scuffling in the distance and a movement in the undergrowth. I called out, just in case, "Marcie?" There was no reply, so I tried instead, "Flame! Here, girl!"

I heard a muffled voice from the phone in my hand and I spoke into it. "Seriously, Miles. Hold

156

on. I think I've got her."

He said something, but it was drowned out by the sound of Cisco's sharp bark. The leash had gone slack in my hand.

"Weird," I murmured. Cisco had been trained to sit and bark when he found his search object, but the search object was generally static—an injured victim or an inanimate object. A runaway border collie wasn't the kind of target he would give the "find" signal for, unless... unless the dog was injured and unable to move. "Oh, no," I said and started to run.

"Where are you?" Miles demanded. "I'm coming that way."

My breath hissed and gasped into the receiver as I clambered over fallen saplings and broken rocks to where Cisco, half-disguised by the shadow of foliage, sat and barked again. I managed, "Wait, it's okay." And then I sucked in my breath, stumbling to a stop.

"Oh God," I whispered.

"Raine? Raine, are you okay?"

I couldn't answer. Cisco was sitting, as he'd been trained to do, looking anxious and alert beside Flame. Flame was lying down, head between her paws, staring fixedly at something half-concealed in the undergrowth. That something was a woman's leg.

I moved slowly forward, one step and two, and then sank to my knees when they would no longer support me. For the longest time all I could do was stare at the Golden Retriever Club of America sweatshirt, streaked with blood and loamy earth, matted with crushed leaves. Gently, I reached forward and pushed a clump of tangled hair away from a face that was so swollen and disfigured it was barely recognizable. I felt for a pulse with shaking fingers but knew already it was pointless.

"Miles," I said hoarsely, "hang up and call 9-1-1. It's Marcie. I think… I think she's dead."

CHAPTER TWELVE

Five hours before the shooting

Buck stopped by the office at change of shift, as was his habit. Even on his rare Saturdays off—of which this was not one—he liked to get a report from the night shift and check for bulletins or updates that might have come in on the computer overnight. This time of year things were pretty quiet around the county; the kids were still in school and the tourists hadn't started getting lost in the woods or running their cars off a cliff, and if anything major had happened while he was away someone would have called. Still, he liked to check.

"Four DUIs, two domestics, one B and E," reported Ham Broker, his night Charge Officer. "Turns out it was the complainant's son, trying to sneak back into the house after curfew. Syd Evans ran his car into a tree over on Blue Moon Trail, but he's okay. The man's blind as a bat after dark. We're going to have to do something before he hurts himself."

"Sounds like a light night for a Friday," Buck said. He glanced through the duty log on the way to his office. He called good morning to the guys who were filling their coffee cups and good night to the ones who were just leaving.

"You know what else we need to do," Ham said, following him.

"Hire two new deputies."

"At least. One good case of flu and this county will be wide open."

"I'm working on it, Ham." Because he knew that sounded a little short, he glanced up and added, "I appreciate the job you boys are doing."

Ham rubbed his cheek wearily. "Ah, ▓▓▓▓ Buck, we know you're doing the best you can. It's just with tourist season coming on and some of the guys are worried about vacation time…"

Buck said, trying for that just right note between patient understanding and confident authority that Roe always used to master so effortlessly, "I know. I'm working on it."

Ham looked as though he wanted to say something else, but settled for, "Well, I'm ready for some shut-eye. Oh, Rosie said before she left last night to make sure you saw that." He gestured to a printout on top of Buck's desk. "An APB on some fellow by the name of Jeremiah Berman. Came in after you left yesterday afternoon. She said you'd tagged him."

The Hanover County Sherriff's Department was routinely notified of all APBs in the tri-state area because of their proximity to the junction of North Carolina, South Carolina, and Tennessee. The sheer numbers would have been overwhelming, so only those alerts with a specific reference to Western North Carolina—or those that had been specifically requested by law enforcement in the area—were directed to the Sheriff's Department inbox. After learning of Berman's parole violation yesterday, Buck had put in a routine request for an alert if and when his name came up in the system. He hadn't expected such a quick response.

There was such a jumble of papers on his desk that Rosie had taken to flagging the important ones with red sticky notes. Now there were so many red sticky notes that the word "urgent" had lost its meaning. Buck scrambled among the papers until he found the printout of the computerized bulletin and scanned it quickly.

"Looks like he drove off without paying at a gas pump in South Carolina," Ham supplied. "The police traced the plates and found they were stolen. Parole violation, theft by taking, armed and dangerous."

The printout included two camera shots: one of a thin-faced man with a scraggly beard, the official prison ID photo, and the other of a six-year-old blue Chevy pickup truck. Unfortunately for Berman, the angle of the camera also clearly showed the presence of an M14 rifle casually stored behind the passenger seat. Failure to report to his parole officer was one thing. Possession of a firearm while in commission of a crime was something else altogether. And Buck couldn't help noticing the irony of the fact that the technology that might have proven Berman's innocence twenty years ago was now going to send him back to prison for what might be a very long time indeed.

"Do we need to keep a lookout for this fellow, Sheriff?"

Buck frowned as he read the paper. "Killianville?" he said. "That's nowhere around here, is it?"

"Nah, it's farther toward the coast. You're

headed toward Charleston, you'll see exits for Surreytown, Killianville, Pembroke. Two hundred miles away, easy."

Buck relaxed. "Well, that's something anyway." He slid behind the desk and unlocked his computer, still puzzling over the printout. "Why ~~the hell~~ South Carolina?"

Ham said uncertainly, "Something we need to know, Sheriff?"

"Hmm?" Buck tapped the Enter key impatiently, urging the screen to come up. He glanced at Ham absently. "No. Nothing yet. Get some sleep, Ham. Tell Adele hi for me, okay?"

"Yes, sir. Okay, will do. Have a good day now."

But Buck was already deep into the information on the screen, and he didn't even notice when Ham left.

He was still researching updates when his cell phone rang ten minutes later. He glanced at the caller ID and answered with, "Hey. Listen to this. Berman apparently left Georgia yesterday after 'borrowing' his brother's pickup truck with an M14 in the back. Changed license plates somewhere in South Carolina and stole a tank of gas late last night in Killianville. Abandoned the truck in a mall outside of Pembroke, where we can assume he picked up another car. The rifle wasn't found."

Wyn said, "Good morning. I love you too."

He winced and refocused. "Hey, hon. I'm sorry. I can't get this thing off my mind."

"That's okay. Actually, great minds obsess alike. I had an idea after we talked last night. Remember we sent Smokey Beardsley upstate for possession five years ago? I did an inmate search, and guess where he ended up? Marion Correctional Institute, same as his old buddy Berman. Now, I'm not saying they were cozying up together or anything, but what do you think the chances are that the two of them didn't get together to talk about old times?"

Buck sat up straighter. "Damn it, you're right. Smokey got out last spring. He's been keeping his nose clean, more or less…"

Wyn gave a disbelieving sniff. "As far as anyone can tell."

"But if a guy like Berman wanted a contact on the outside…"

"It might be worth a trip down a dirt road to talk to him."

Buck closed his eyes slowly. "Damn," he said. "I miss you."

"Always just a phone call away," she returned

brightly.

"And seventy-two miles."

"Well, there's that."

After a silence, he said, "What are you doing today?"

"Buying oranges, getting my hair cut, going for a run, doing laundry. You?"

"Talking to Smokey Beardsley." He hesitated. "Not too short."

"What?"

"Your hair. I like it long."

She laughed. "Later, alligator."

"Hey," he said. "Good morning. And I love you."

Her voice was soft. "Back at you, big guy."

She disconnected with a click, and he was once again alone with the computer screen.

Everyone gathered in the far corner of the parking lot, the one nearest the woods, and watched the coroner's van take Marcie away. There was a crime scene van, three police cars, two detectives, two hotel security guards, and a growing contingent of hotel guests with their dogs.

Donna Ball

A frantic hotel manager with spiked blond hair kept a cell phone pressed to his ear while he paced back and forth, and a couple waitresses from the dining room brought trays of coffee and Danish, their eyes big with curiosity and dread. A portion of the field and the parking lot had been taped off, and most of the curious onlookers were kept on the far side of that tape. Those of us who were considered material witnesses, however, were confined inside the barrier. I wasn't sure which was worse.

The detective said, "So you were walking your dog this morning when you found the victim in the woods. Is that correct?"

I wasn't sure how many times I'd repeated my story. I wasn't sure how many times I'd have to repeat it before they got it right.

"No," I said. I felt Miles's hand on my shoulder, gently kneading the knots that were tightening at the base of my neck. I took a breath and spoke more calmly. "The victim's—Marcie's—dog was running loose. My dog is a trained search dog. He tracked the runaway dog. But it was her dog, Flame, who led us to her."

"Is that a fact?" The detective looked up from his notebook, appearing interested. "A trained

166

search dog, huh?"

"We're with Mountain Wilderness Search and Rescue," I explained wearily. "Western North Carolina."

He pursed his lips in a way that was meant to indicate he was impressed. "So what are you doing down this way?"

"There's a dog show."

He glanced around at all the dogs and uneasy-looking handlers gathered both inside and outside the taped barrier. "No kidding? My wife has a poodle. She always talked about showing it."

"This isn't that kind of dog show."

I glanced down at Cisco, who'd grown bored with all the standing around and was lying at my feet. Miles had wanted to take him back to the room, particularly at the height of all the excitement and confusion, but he clearly didn't understand how it was with us. My hand was melded to the leash now. Without the warmth of Cisco's body heat against my foot, I would've felt like a part of me was missing. And I wasn't the only one. None of the women who gathered around with such anxious, disbelieving looks on their faces had seen fit to leave their dogs in the car. When you're scared, you want your best friend with you. That's just the way it is.

Miles said, "Someone called Raine's room last night trying to get her to come to the front desk. You'll find a complaint on record with the night manager. It looks as though someone was trying to lure women from their rooms in the middle of the night."

Of course, in the horror of the moment, the whole story of the call in the night, as well as the story of the man who'd tried to sneak into the building under Sarah's key card, had come tumbling out. The white line that appeared around Miles's lips when I finished telling it was still visible.

I repeated the story of the incident now to the detective, who took it down dutifully. When I finished, he said, "Yes, I have a statement already from a Sarah Lissick about the man who tried to get into the building. Her description was fairly general, but it was something to go on at least."

I swallowed hard. "Marcie wasn't at dinner when we were talking about it. We all agreed to walk our dogs in the courtyard last night, but Marcie didn't know."

The detective said, "Thank you, Ms. Stockton. I think we have everything we need now. We have your cell phone number if we have any more questions."

"What about her boyfriend?" Miles said. "Neil…"

He glanced at me questioningly, and I supplied, "Neil Kellog."

"He seemed pretty upset when he was arguing with her yesterday," Miles said, "and more than capable of violence. I heard him threaten her. Someone should talk to him."

"He's on our list," the detective assured him.

I said, "They were arguing about the dog, Bryte. Neil wanted to take her home, but yesterday afternoon when Marcie came back to the hotel, she had Bryte with her. And there was a man with her too. I don't know who he was."

The detective was taking notes again, but I was concerned with more immediate matters. "Someone needs to get the dogs home. Does anyone know who's supposed to be in charge of the dogs?"

A member of the hotel staff had unlocked Marcie's room at the request of the police, and poor Bryte was finally freed. Who knew how long she'd been locked in there alone, barking for help? I volunteered to put both dogs in my SUV until someone made a decision about what to do with them.

The medical examiner said the cause of death was most likely strangulation, although the bruises and lacerations on her body suggested she'd been badly beaten first. I hadn't heard her give a time of death, but it wasn't hard to figure out. Marcie had been wearing the same clothes she'd worn yesterday, so it was probable she'd been lying out in the woods all night. Of course, she might have gotten up this morning and put on the same outfit just as I had done, but I had a different theory. At dinner she'd mentioned Flame had an upset stomach. She must have taken her out sometime last night, and she'd never come back. When the assailant grabbed Marcie, she would have dropped the leash, and Flame got away. The poor dog spent the entire night running in hopeless terror, looking for help, until she'd spotted Cisco and me this morning. And even then, we hadn't understood what she'd been trying to tell us. Or at least I hadn't.

When I travel, I keep an emergency contact form for my dogs right next to the emergency contact information on myself, so whoever is in charge of taking care of me will know who to call to come get my dogs. Maude would drive any distance for my dogs, and so would Buck if it came to that, so those are the numbers I list, along with specific instructions that my dogs are not to be taken to an animal shelter and a promise to pay any boarding or vet fees that accrue. Why doesn't everyone do that? And why doesn't the premium form for every dog event require you to give specific instructions for the disposition of your dog in case you're incapacitated?

My mind was wandering, and I almost missed the detective's question.

The detective said, "Can you describe him?"

I blinked, surprised to feel the hot wetness in my eyes. "Who?"

Miles squeezed my shoulder reassuringly and pressed another paper cup of coffee into my hand. I said, "Oh. The man. He was tall, light-haired. Broad-shouldered. I didn't see his face. I got the impression they were close. Marcie seemed upset and he comforted her. I thought he might be staying here with her, but I guess not."

"Had you ever seen him before?"

"No. But I'd never seen Marcie before yesterday, either. Someone who knows her could probably identify him."

"But he wasn't with her when you saw her at dinner last night?"

I shook my head. "I didn't think it was my place to ask about him. Like I said, I didn't know her that well."

The detective said, "Thank you for your help, Ms. Stockton." He handed me a business card. "We'll be in touch if we need anything more."

I said, "If I were you, I'd check the emergency rooms for dog bite cases."

He looked puzzled and I explained, "If she was walking her dog when she was abducted, the man probably had to fight off Flame. Her dog. Border collies can be nervous. They have a reputation for biting first and apologizing later when they're threatened." I shrugged. "Just an idea."

He nodded thoughtfully. "Not a bad one. I'll put someone on it."

He moved away and Cisco stood and stretched, ready now to get on with his day. Miles kept his hand on my back as we left the cordoned-off area, lifting the tape for Cisco and me to duck under. "Why don't you give Cisco some breakfast and get your things packed?" he said. "I'll settle the bill."

It's funny how the mind works. I wasn't *really* planning to go to the fairgrounds and run jumpers-with-weaves today as though finding a fellow competitor murdered in the woods was just a minor interruption to my schedule, but for some reason I hadn't considered not going, either. I certainly hadn't planned to just pack up and go home.

"Do you mean—check out?"

"You certainly don't intend to stay here." It wasn't a question. "In fact, I'd be very surprised if any of the guests do once they know what happened." He slipped his arm around my waist in a brief hug. "Tell you what. We'll drive down to the beach, get an ocean-front suite, take Cisco for a run—they allow dogs on the beach until May—and I know this great place for dinner right on the waterfront. Mel's flight doesn't get in until eight tomorrow night, so we still have most of the weekend."

I said, "I don't want to go to the beach."

His hand slid away from my waist. "Well, you're not staying here."

It didn't matter how right he was; there's something about being told what I will and will not do that has always set my teeth on edge. "I'm a grown woman. I can stay wherever I want to."

Those gorgeous gray eyes of his can be as hard

as flint when the circumstances dictate. I felt chilled just looking at them. "Do you remember when you were talking earlier about having important things to fight about? This is one of them."

"Oh, for heaven's sake, Miles." I turned on my heel, and he grabbed my arm. Cisco barked once, sharply. Had Flame barked like that last night when a stranger grabbed Marcie in the dark?

I pulled my arm away from Miles and dropped my hand quickly to Cisco's head. My sweet dog looked embarrassed to have let his nerves, which had to be as edgy as mine, get away with him. "It's okay, boy."

Cisco shook himself, grinned, and by way of apology, raised himself on his back paws and placed his front paws on Miles's torso. Miles obligingly rubbed his shoulders, but his eyes were unsmiling on mine. "Talk some sense into her, will you, fellow?"

Cisco bounced all four paws on the ground and looked up at me with anxious eyes, possibly hoping I would remember his breakfast, possibly sensing, in the way dogs have, the discord between the two humans who were responsible for his care and hoping for nothing more than peace. I could have used a little peace myself at that moment.

174

Miles said, making an obvious effort to moderate his tone, "Okay, how about this? Let's get Cisco situated and then talk about it over breakfast."

"I can't eat anything. I'm going to throw up."

A faint smile traced the corners of his lips. "You're not going to throw up. You're my hero."

I tried to smile back and couldn't manage it.

Miles said, very quietly, "She was wearing your sweatshirt, Raine. When I looked at her... it could have been you. If you had listened to that jerk on the phone last night, if you had left your room..."

I felt my throat clutch. "I would never leave my room in the middle of the night."

"Are you kidding me?" The anger was back. "You do it all the time. You've done it twice since I've been here!"

"But I always have Cisco—"

I broke off at the flare of infuriated exasperation in his eyes, because I knew what he was thinking: Marcie had Flame, too. Just like the rest of us, she felt safe with her dog.

I shifted my gaze away, embarrassed and defensive and deeply uncomfortable. "Do what you have to," I mumbled. "I have Marcie's dogs in my car. I need to make arrangements for them."

"Does that mean you're leaving with me?"

Strong emotion, especially when I don't understand it, often makes me say stupid things. I snapped back, "I didn't come here with you, did I?"

A woman's voice spoke behind me. "Excuse me, ma'am?"

Someone touched my shoulder lightly and I spun around. "What?"

I found myself looking at a well-groomed and perfectly made-up young woman with a microphone in her hand. Behind her was a much less well-groomed young man in baggy jeans and a tee shirt with a camera mounted to his shoulder. She said pleasantly. "Carolina Mays from WCGA News." She pronounced it Caro*leen*a. "Are you the person who found the victim?"

As I might have mentioned, I'm used to being interviewed, and so is Cisco. I said, "That's right."

"Do you mind talking with us about it, Ms.…."

"Stockton," I supplied. "Raine Stockton."

Cisco sat beautifully at my side and I saw the camera guy lower his shot to focus on my dog. That was good. At this hour of the morning, I was no competition for Cisco in a beauty contest.

The reporter said, "I understand you were

walking your dog when you came upon the body in the woods."

I sighed and began the story again. "No. My dog is a trained search dog…"

The interview took five or six minutes and included several close-ups of Cisco's intelligent golden face, which I knew would be reduced to ten seconds on the noon news. When the reporter and cameraman moved off in search of other interviewees, I turned back to Miles, but he was gone.

It probably shouldn't have surprised me that Ginny and Aggie were a veritable font of information for the police, and Sarah, of course, was interviewed extensively about the incident with the man who tried to follow her into the building. I waited until Aggie was in between interviews and waved her over.

"How are you holding up?" she insisted, squeezing my arm. "What an awful thing. I can't believe we were almost out of the parking lot when we saw the ambulance. We wouldn't have known what happened until we got back tonight! And then it would be too late to find another hotel.

Someone needs to tell the people who've already gone to the fairgrounds. I texted the trial secretary, but I haven't heard anything back. I can't imagine anyone will feel safe here tonight. I know Ginny and I are going straight home after the competition today. No ribbon is worth this. Are you okay? I'd have nightmares for the rest of my life."

I said, "Do you know what Marcie would want us to do with the dogs? Does she have any relatives or anyone who would come get them?"

Aggie frowned. "Oh, dear. Well, there's Neil, of course. He is the co-owner of the dogs."

We looked at each other, but there really was no need to say it. Nonetheless, Aggie did, albeit in a much lower tone. "Of course, since he's probably going to end up in jail…"

"We don't know that."

"Oh, honey, you were right there yesterday when they had that big fight, and everybody heard him threaten her! And that's not even the worst. Why, Marcie told me…"

I said firmly, "I'm sure the police will get to the bottom of what happened to Marcie. In the meantime, Neil is the legal co-owner of the dogs and he's the one we need to contact. Do you know how to reach him? The contact name on the dogs' tags is Marcie's."

She still looked reluctant. "He was supposed to run Bryte this afternoon. I guess you could try him at home, but…"

"You don't happen to know where I could find his number?"

"No, but Marcie said he has a place in town. He shouldn't be too hard to find." She shook her head sadly. "It's just so unbelievable. Maybe someone in the club knows if she has any relatives. I'm sure someone is taking care of her other dogs back home. Ginny and I will ask around when we get to the fairgrounds and see if anyone has any ideas. But if all else fails, we'll be glad to take the dogs home with us and keep them until things are settled. You know, in case Neil can't."

"That would be great. I know her family will appreciate that. Meanwhile, though, I think I should try to find Neil."

Aggie nodded agreement and returned a wan smile. "If the police don't find him first."

CHAPTER THIRTEEN

Four hours, fourteen minutes before the shooting

Buck found Smokey sitting in front of his trailer in a folding metal chair, drinking a beer. It was only ten in the morning, and Buck was surprised to find him awake. He left the squad car parked behind a rusted-out Pontiac and a Jesus van on blocks and picked his way around a smattering of old tires, metal fire barrels, the remnants of a sofa, and an electric stove without an oven door. He kept a wary eye out for Smokey's pit bull, who had a tendency to charge first and bark later, and rested his hand on his gun holster, just so Smokey could see it.

When he was ten or fifteen feet away, he stopped and called, "Morning, Smokey. Where's your dog?"

Smokey had let himself go to seed since getting out of prison, not that he'd been much of a fashion model before that. He had a gut on him that wasn't flattered by the stained wife beater tee shirt and motor-oil splattered jeans he wore, and the scrub of beard that sagged on his face was bristled with gray. He narrowed his bloodshot eyes, drank from the can, and replied when he was ready. "Dead." He had a long, low bayou accent—his people were from the swamp country of Louisiana—that made the word sound like "dayid." He spat on the ground and added, "Got hisself rattlesnake bit last August."

"Sorry to hear that." Buck proceeded toward the trailer.

"You got issue with me, officer?"

"Just a friendly visit." Buck looked around until he found a plastic lawn chair that looked as though it would hold him and tilted it forward to drain a puddle of water leftover from the rain shower two days ago. He found a level place in the ground a few feet away from Smokey and set the chair there. He sat down, noticing as he did a flutter of the ragged dishtowel that served as a window curtain behind him. "Who's in the house?"

"Nobody."

"Ask Nobody to come out."

Smokey glared at him for a minute, then bellowed over his shoulder, "Jolene! Bring me another beer!"

In a moment the front door opened and a horse-faced woman in an ill-fitting house dress and animal print slippers came out. She kept a suspicious eye on Buck as she moved past him, giving his chair a wide berth, to hand Smokey the can of beer she brought. Nonetheless, Buck half rose in his chair and gave her a polite nod. "Morning, ma'am."

"I didn't do nothin'," she muttered and scuttled back into the trailer. Buck heard the lock click on the door when she closed it.

Smokey drained the first beer, crumpled it in his fist, and dropped it on the ground. He popped the tab on the second. "That all you come out here for, Deputy? To see who was in my house and what happened to my dog?"

Buck let the mistake in his title slide. Smokey had been away for a while and didn't know, or care, about his promotion. In a way, that was a good thing. "Just being cautious," he replied. "Considering the last time I was out here you pulled a gun on me, I figured that'd be smart."

Smokey grunted. "I had a right."

"I reckon."

Smokey took a long draw of his beer. "You got something to say to me, you'd best get on with sayin' it. I got things to do."

Buck said, "I've always been fair with you, haven't I, Smokey?"

The other man drank his beer, not looking at him, not talking.

"I never hunted you when I could have. I never hassled you over small stuff, and I let one or two things slide when you know well and good I could've put you in County for a month or two if I'd ever had a mind to."

Still, Smokey said nothing.

"So all that considered, I thought there might not be any harm in a couple of old friends like us having a conversation."

"I got friends. You ain't one of them."

"All right. Acquaintances, then. How'd you like it upstate at Marion?"

Smokey slithered a beady glance at him, held it steady for a minute, and then looked away. "Wadn't so bad. No picnic, but I'm here, ain't I?"

"Make any new friends? Maybe get reacquainted with some old ones?"

Smokey said nothing.

"Do you remember a fellow by the name of Jeremiah Allen Berman?"

Smokey sucked on his beer, and Buck waited patiently. At last he said, "So what if I do?"

"Just thought you might've run into him upstate. I was wondering if he ever said anything to you about coming back here. About maybe having some unfinished business."

Smokey gazed fixedly at the right fender of the rusted out Pontiac, swiping his tongue around the rim of the can, gathering dew. "Don't know why a man'd ever want to come back to this godforsaken butt crack at the end of the earth if'n he didn't have to."

"I'm just asking."

Once again, Smokey slid him a bloody-eyed look. "You gunnin' for him?"

Buck shrugged. "He hasn't done anything to me."

The look turned speculative. "But if you was, and if I was to help you out somehows, you reckon you'd be grateful to ol' Smokey?"

Buck's gaze was steady. "As grateful as I'm allowed to be."

Smokey held his stare for another moment and

then gave a short, surprising burst of cackling laughter. "Ain't nothin' to me nohow," he said. "That was one pe-culiar bird. Beat this one girl half to death down in Georgia, raped her, stuffed her in the trunk of his car, then drove her out to the lake and tossed her in, still alive. Least that's the story he told. Everybody knew it. Did you know it?"

"I wasn't around back then."

"He liked to tell stories about what he'd got away with. He got away with a lot." He drank. "But upstate, now, he got smart. Smart like a fox, you know what I mean? Knew how to play the system. Signed up for these computer classes in vo-hab. Said he was gonna make something of hisself. Even went to chapel sometimes. That's what the smart ones do. They play the system. But he was still one pe-culiar-~~mean~~ bird."

"How's that?"

"Carried around a picture of a dead guy, for one. Tore it out of a newspaper and had it so long it was all sweaty and crumpled and about to fall apart. But he'd take it out now and then and just look at it with this real scary grin on his face, mutterin' to hisself. Always said the same thing."

"What did he say?"

"Something church-like. Lemme think."

Smokey licked the rim of the can again. "Sins of the father, that's it. 'Sins of the father, you ~~somethin'~~ ~~~~ was what he was sayin', over and over again. 'Sins of the father.'"

Buck frowned. "That picture. Do you know who it was?"

Smokey shrugged. "Some judge is all I know." He drained the beer, crumpled the can, and dropped it on the ground beside the other. "Said it was the judge that sent him up."

Miles was leaning against the driver's door of my SUV as I came around the corner of the parking lot, his expression unreadable. I watched him carefully as I approached.

"So," he said, "where are we going?"

I unlocked the doors with a click of the remote control. "I thought you were checking out."

"And I thought you were packing."

"I told you, I have to find someone to take care of these dogs."

"Let me guess. The guy with the temper and the fancy footwork who, less than twenty-four hours ago, threatened both you and the woman they just took to the morgue."

Sometimes I really hate it when he outthinks me. Sometimes it saves me a lot of explaining. So I replied defiantly, "That's right."

"Do you have his address?"

I had done a search on my smartphone, and only one Neil Kellog came up in Pembroke. I said, "Yes."

"You couldn't just have called him, I suppose."

I could have, but I wanted to see him. I wanted to look into his eyes when I told him about Marcie, and if I didn't like what I saw there, nothing could make me leave those dogs with him.

Miles pushed away from the door. "I'll drive. You navigate."

He held out his hand for the keys, and after a moment, I gave them to him.

I secured Cisco in his seat belt in the back seat, and the two border collies in the cargo area poked their black-tipped noses over the barrier curiously. When all the dogs had greeted each other and I was certain everyone was comfortable, I got into the passenger seat beside Miles and brought up the driving directions on my phone. "Right turn out of the parking lot," I said. "Then left on Burke Boulevard for six miles."

He made the left, easily navigating the Saturday morning traffic with one hand on the steering wheel. Cisco curled up in the bench seat behind me and closed his eyes. The border collies were quiet.

Miles said, "My first wife was gorgeous."

I glared at him in disbelief, then slumped down in my seat with my arms crossed over my chest. "Thanks a lot."

"Not as gorgeous as you, of course," he continued smoothly, "but a head-turner nonetheless. That would have been okay, but she also had this tendency to flirt. I knew it was harmless, but other men would misread her. We use to go out dancing—"

I looked at him in surprise. "I didn't know you liked to dance."

"Oh yeah. I'm a hell of a salsa dancer. Do a mean boot-scoot, too. The point is, she would dance with anyone who asked her, and I would spend most of the night feeling like a bouncer, waiting for somebody to get out of line. I didn't mind if she danced with other guys. I wanted her to have a good time. But she never understood that, while she was out there bringing down the house, I was the one who was in danger of getting my teeth knocked out every time some drunk put his hand in the wrong place. Women just don't get it. They go off half-cocked with some reckless scheme or another and never think about how it affects the man who's trying to protect her."

Miles rarely talked about his ex-wives, and we'd been on the verge of having a nice moment. Now I bristled. "I don't want or *need* protecting, thank you very much!"

"Doesn't matter. That's the thing you don't get. Men can't help it. We're hardwired to protect the women we care about, and whether you like it or not, somebody's been doing it for you all your life. Your dad, your uncle, every boyfriend you've ever had, your husband. Whether you mean to or not, whether you want to or not, every time you put yourself at risk you're putting some man who cares about you in danger. And since men are essentially selfish beasts who value our creature comforts, that ~~pisses~~ us off. Which way?"

We'd come to a stop sign, but I was so disconcerted by what he'd said that for a moment I'd forgotten what we were doing here. I glanced at the map on my phone and said, "Left on Randolph Street, then right on High Manor Way."

I let the street signs roll by silently while I

absorbed his words. I'd never thought about it that way before, but deep inside I knew he was right. And I felt bad for it. I said quietly, "I can't change who I am, Miles."

"I know that. I'm still around, aren't I? But if I raise my voice now and then, that's why." He reached across the seat and squeezed my knee. "Hey, I like cave diving and parasailing, neither one of which endears me to my insurance carrier. So maybe that's something we have in common."

I stared at him. "Stupidity?"

He laughed and then made the turn into a wide, neatly maintained street lined with white brick apartment buildings. "Looks like this is it. What's the number?"

"Two forty-six, apartment A." I hesitated. "Probably best if you let me do the talking. I mean, don't mention the dogs."

"Because you're not really going to leave them with him."

I slid a glance his way. Like I said, sometimes he saves me a lot of time explaining. "I just want to talk to him. He probably knows by now he's under investigation. If he really values the dogs—and I know he does—he'll have a plan for someone to take care of them."

We pulled into a parking space next to a dusty red SUV with a border collie sticker in the rear window and a bumper sticker that read "Faster Than a Speeding Border Collie." I could see dog crates in the back. Miles left the windows cracked for the dogs, even though the morning was still cool, and we got out of the car in front of Neil's apartment building. Cisco pressed his nose through the opening in the back window, looking offended to be left behind, and I smiled at him. Then I said to Miles, "Hey."

He glanced at me.

"Thanks for coming with me."

He smiled then and dropped his hand to my shoulder. "You're buying breakfast," he said.

We went up the walk and I pressed the buzzer to apartment A. While we waited for an answer, I looked at Miles and said, "So what happened to wife number one?"

He shrugged. "She got tired of flirting. I got tired of fighting. We both moved on to bigger and better things."

I pushed the bell again. We waited.

Miles said, "Maybe he's not here."

I nodded toward the parking lot. "That has to be his car."

He looked at me meaningfully. "Maybe the police got here before us."

I frowned and punched the bell again. We waited.

Miles said, "You don't think he did it, do you?"

"No, I don't."

"The dog, right?'

"Right. He knows how valuable she is. He trained her from a pup. He wouldn't just let her run loose like that." I could see skepticism in his eyes, so I added, "You have to know dog people."

Miles knocked loudly on the door. "There aren't too many lawyers who could win with the you-have-to-know-dog-people defense, so I hope this guy has an alibi. And I hope you have a backup plan, because it doesn't look like he's home."

He started to turn away, but I held up a hand. "Wait. I think I hear someone inside." I knocked again. "Neil?" I called. "Neil, are you there? I want to talk to you about Bryte and Flame."

A chain rattled on the inside, there was some fumbling with the doorknob, and the door swung open. Neil leaned against the doorframe, blinking at us slowly in the gentle morning light, his pupils the size of dimes. His hair was crumpled and his complexion pasty, and his right hand was wrapped in a heavy gauze bandage. I barely noticed any of this, though. I was too busy staring at the blood spatters on his tee shirt.

CHAPTER FOURTEEN

Three hours, forty-six minutes before the shooting

N eil said, "Who ▓▓ ▓▓▓ are you?" His voice was thick and somewhat slurred, and he swayed a little on his feet. I noticed for the first time that he was propped up by a crutch and the right leg of his jeans was neatly split from thigh to ankle, revealing a heavy white cast at the knee.

I said, completely disoriented, "Um... maybe we've come at a bad time..."

"I'm Miles Young and this is my friend Raine Stockton," Miles said, speaking over me. "We met yesterday at the dog trial, but you probably don't remember. We'll just come in for a minute. Here, let me give you a hand there. Looks like you had a rough night."

Miles urged me forward with a firm hand on my back, and I couldn't help staring at him as I stepped over the threshold. Sometimes the guy can really surprise me.

All Miles murmured in response was, "We came this far. You weren't really planning to leave, were you?" Then he turned to Neil, assisting him with the crutch. "These things can be tricky. There you go."

We entered a living room that was dark and sparsely furnished: a couch, a flat screen, a bean bag chair, and a small plastic, outdoor-type table that held a laptop, a stack of *Clean Run* magazines, and some empty beer cans. It smelled, as most bachelor apartments do, of dirty laundry and stale pizza. Neil, with Miles's help, collapsed on the brown-striped sofa, and I glanced around until I located the kitchen. I rinsed out a glass from the pile of dishes in the sink, and filled it with water. I heard Neil saying, "Who are you again? ███████ painkillers."

I brought him the water and sat gingerly on the far end of the couch, leaning forward to remain in his line of sight. Miles sat on the arm of the sofa beside me. "What happened to you?" I asked, and my concern was genuine. "Are you going to be okay?"

He focused on me with the effort of a swimmer pushing his way to the surface. "I know you," he said at last. "You're the one who caught Bryte yesterday. I didn't thank you. I'm sorry. Yesterday… was a ▉▉▉ of a day."

"That's okay," I assured him. "Is this…"—I gestured to his knee—"because of the fall you took yesterday?"

He looked at me for a moment, slow to comprehend, and then gave a short bark of laughter. "In a way." He took a thirsty gulp of the water. "Look, I just spent twelve hours in the emergency room. I already told the police everything I know. You said something about my dogs. Are they okay?" A sudden alarm brought cognizance to his eyes, and he pushed himself forward, wincing at the pain. "He didn't try to hurt them, did he? She didn't let him get to them?"

I said quickly, "Flame and Bryte are fine." He sank back against the sofa, and I added, "Who? Who would try to hurt them?'

"The same guy that did this to me." He closed his eyes. "Big fellow, blond hair, gray shirt. I told the police. ████, my head is spinning. I can't keep them here. He might come back. I've got to talk to Marcie."

I glanced at Miles. Sometimes I can read his mind, too. I let him say it. "So the police have already been here…"

He dragged a hand over his face, as though trying to reestablish circulation. "Yeah. Last night. Yesterday. Some time, I don't know. I told them I'd never seen the guy before. I opened the door and he pushed his way in here, swinging a lead pipe. Broke my hand, then my knee. Then he said something like, 'That ought to do it,' and walked out of here as calm as you please while I lay there screaming on the floor. ████████."

"What about Bryte?" I said. "You said you were taking her home with you yesterday. Was she still here?"

He shook his head and fumbled for the water glass. "I never got her out of the fairgrounds. Marcie promised we'd work out a deal after the trial. I guess…" He took another gulp of water. "This is it."

I looked at Miles in confusion. He gave me a silent shrug.

I said, "What time was all this?"

"I don't know. Four o'clock, maybe. It was almost dark by the time the ambulance got here. I kept passing out trying to get to the phone."

I was really hurting for the poor guy, but Miles was more practical. "And you just got out of the hospital this morning?"

He nodded and took another drink of water. "They wanted to keep me a few days, but I don't have insurance, and…" He shrugged. "The dog training business doesn't exactly make you rich."

"Tell me about it," I murmured sympathetically.

"That's why I couldn't really blame Marcie for what she did." He went on, talking now almost as though to himself. "But to borrow money from people like that… Her problem is that just because she's got a law degree, she thinks she knows everything. The main thing she knows is how to wiggle in and out of the law without getting caught, if you ask me. I always knew there was something a little off about the way she did business and who she did it with, but I never thought she'd risk the dogs." His voice fell a bit. "I don't think she meant to, not really. That doesn't make it right, what she did, but even she has limits. She couldn't have known it would come to this."

I was completely lost, but Miles seemed relatively unsurprised. "So Marcie got in over her head, borrowed money from these, er, business associates…"

"She helped them put together some kind of deal. They said if she ever needed a favor… She said she didn't know it would get so complicated, but how stupid could she be? She knew what kind of animals they were."

"And you think that's somehow related to what happened to you last night?"

"Think?" He gave a dry snort of disgust. "I know. She as much as told me so yesterday. These dudes are into some seriously sleazy stuff. Video gambling, prostitution, loan sharking, all kinds of racketeering… They killed one guy that tried to narc on them over in Surreytown."

I twisted around to stare at Miles. His face was unreadable. "So let me guess," he said. "They kept raising the interest, she couldn't pay…"

"Nah, it wasn't the money they wanted. It was the win. The dogs. I was the trainer. She was in charge of everything else. She ran this game like a business. For her, I guess it was. She said that's the way to win. Maybe she was right."

"So," I said carefully, trying to understand,

"these people, these bad people, they wanted your winnings from the Standard Cup?"

"Not just that," Miles answered for him, and Neil didn't object. "They were manipulating the odds on all the dogs, all the competitions. That's the way racketeering works."

"I didn't know what she was into, just that nothing good was going to come of it for me. We have a contract on Flame about sharing the profits, but not on Bryte. So I figured if I blew the run with Flame, I'd be out of our agreement, and whatever I won with Bryte would be mine. Like I said, I didn't know what kind of people she was mixed up with. She broke down and told me everything yesterday afternoon, and I was furious, of course. I just wanted to take Bryte and get out of there, but I'd never seen her so scared. After she almost lost Bryte, after you caught her, she begged me to help her, to hang on for just a little while longer. She promised she had a plan, and it would all be over in a matter of days if I'd just cooperate. We'd been together for a long time. I didn't know what else to do. I said I'd go through with the rest of the trial and we'd figure something out. Guess somebody else figured something out first."

I felt as though I was on a speeding train, with

pieces of the puzzle flashing past like scraps of scenery through a window. "But," I managed, "you left the dogs with her. How could you do that?"

"The dogs are assets," Miles assured me. "They wouldn't hurt the dogs."

It seemed to me that Neil had been an asset, too, but that hadn't protected him. I didn't know what to think, much less say. It all sounded like something out of a B-grade movie, and none of it made sense. None of it. Gangsters, loan sharks, thugs breaking people's kneecaps. Was he hallucinating? Was I? Was it all some kind of very bizarre and not-at-all funny joke?

There was absolutely no sign of mirth on Neil's slightly gray face, and when I glanced at Miles, all I saw in his eyes was dark concern. One thing was certain. If Neil had been in the emergency room all night, he could have had nothing to do with what happened to Marcie. And if any part of what he said was true, the police were by now pursuing a very different tack indeed. While I was sure they would be around to talk to Neil again sometime today, they clearly hadn't been here since taking the report on Marcie's assault. Neil didn't even know his former girlfriend was now lying on a slab in the morgue in what was very likely the same hospital he'd just left.

I took a breath and said, "Listen, Neil, the reason we came here was to tell you that… well, Marcie was in an accident last night."

His eyes opened and he stared at me blearily. Comprehension was vague in his eyes, if present at all. "Accident? Is she okay?"

Oh, I hated this. I shouldn't have to do this. I didn't want to do this. And for once I felt nothing but profound gratitude that a man was there to step in for me and take over.

"She's dead," Miles said gently. "I'm sorry."

Neil swallowed hard, staring at him. "I don't understand."

I really, really didn't see the point in going over the details. I could hardly stand to think about them, and it wasn't my place. I said, "The police are investigating. I'm sure they'll send somebody to talk to you."

"Dead?" he repeated. His hand was shaking as he wiped it over his face, as though trying to clear the fog that clouded his comprehension. "How can she be dead?"

I said, "I'm really so sorry. So sorry you have to hear it like this." Miles placed his hand briefly upon the small of my back in a bracing gesture. I took a breath and plunged on. "What we're trying to find out," I said, "is who is responsible for taking care of the dogs. Since you can't," I added quickly. "Aggie and Ginny from the agility club said they'd drive them back home and keep them until… until someone can come get them, but since you're the co-owner, they need to know if you have another agreement."

He stared at me as though I had spoken Greek. "Marcie's dead?"

I dug into my jeans' pocket, pulled out a couple of pick-up bags, a breath mint, the crumpled remnants of a dog treat, and a wrinkled business card. I looked around until I found a pen, consulted my phone for Aggie's number, and wrote the information on the back of my card. I handed the business card to Neil. "Aggie and Ginny from the agility club," I repeated. "You know them, right?"

He nodded.

"They're going to take care of Bryte and Flame until you feel better."

He stared at the card. "It doesn't make any sense."

I glanced up at Miles, and he simply nodded. We'd done all we could do.

"We're leaving now," I said, standing. "Don't

worry about the dogs."

He didn't look up from the card. "I was going to fix everything. It doesn't make any sense."

Miles and I let ourselves out.

"That was rough," Miles said quietly as we went down the walk.

I drew in a steadying breath. "Yeah." Then I glanced at him. "You were pretty quick to go through that door for someone who was just lecturing me about being reckless."

"Oh, come on, the guy was on crutches. And covered with blood. There was no way I was leaving without finding out how he got that way."

He glanced at me with an expression that couldn't be interpreted as anything but smug as we reached the car. "And by the way, did you notice? I was right."

"You weren't right. It's crazy. Everything he said was crazy."

He opened the car door for me. Cisco sat up in the back seat, grinning to see us, and the two border collies peeked over the barrier. "Where there's money and sports," he said, "there's corruption. It's a rule."

I sank into the seat and tugged on my seat belt. I waited until he was behind the wheel to point out,

"Well, even if it *is* true, it's the Standard Cup that's corrupted, not the AKC."

He started the engine. "That makes a difference?"

I scowled and sank down into my seat. "You bet it does."

I was lost in dark thought until he pulled into the parking lot of a pancake house. By then it was almost lunchtime, and I walked the dogs along the grassy area of the parking lot before we went inside. Miles ordered steak and eggs, and I ordered a grilled cheese sandwich with three orders of steak and eggs to go, hold the salt, hold the gravy, hold the hash browns.

Miles lifted an eyebrow at me. "Sirloin?"

I frowned at him. "The dogs have had a hard day."

He shrugged. "You're paying."

I said, "It doesn't make sense. Assuming, just assuming, there was some kind of mob activity involved—"

He raised a cautionary finger. "Politically incorrect. They prefer 'organized crime.'"

"Why break Neil's knee?" I persisted, ignoring him. "He was the one who could've won the Standard Cup for them. It makes no sense."

"Unless you're betting against him," Miles pointed out.

The waitress brought coffee for him and orange juice for me. I stared at it, wondering why I'd ordered it.

"Look, sweetie," Miles explained, taking out his phone. "In the world of professional sports gambling, there are two ways to win: bet on the winner or bet on the loser. My guess is these guys, whoever they are, figured out Neil wasn't going to play ball a long time ago and put their money on his competitors. His only mistake was planning to run the other dog—Bryte, is it?—for the win."

I stared at him, jaw slackening. "How do you *know* these things?"

He didn't even glance up from the message he was texting. "Remember I told you about my dad, the town drunk? He also played the ponies, among other things. You pick it up here and there."

"Who are you texting?" I demanded in sudden alarm. "You can't—"

He held up a hand for calm. "Mel. She sent a message earlier and I don't want her to worry. Smile, sweetheart."

He pointed the phone at me and I quickly managed a smile and a wave as he snapped the picture. He said, "Check your messages. She copied us both on a group photo in front of the hotel."

I found the photo and texted back a series of hearts and smiley faces. It was the best I could do.

Miles tapped out a few more commands, scrolled a screen or two, and said, "Just like I figured. Bail bonds and DUIs."

I rubbed my forehead, trying to focus. This was an awful lot to take in for someone who only had a couple hours' sleep. "What?"

Miles pocketed his phone and explained. "Most people think all lawyers are automatically rich, but lawyers are a dime a dozen these days, and unless you're in a big city with a big firm, it can be hard to make a living—particularly if you're not very good at it and you have expensive hobbies and high-class tastes. I don't know if you noticed that van she was driving, but it had to be forty, fifty grand."

"Aggie said Marcie has a huge training facility and the property sounds gorgeous," I admitted. "She said their whole club has events there."

"She has a storefront practice in a strip mall that advertises for credit score repair and foreclosure protection, removing DUIs from your record, that kind of thing. Not to say that can't be a lucrative specialty, but it's also the kind of business that's usually done on a cash basis, and where it can be a good idea to have some physical backup when the usual methods of collection aren't effective. So I'm guessing that's how she got involved with these guys and was ready to listen when they came to her with an idea to increase her earnings. I mean, her dogs, with Neil handling them—think of him as the jockey—had been winning for a few years, right? Don't believe for one minute that whatever racket they had going on doesn't go back a decade or so, and they'd been tracking the winners. They didn't want her money. They never do. What they wanted was her assets—the dogs, the handler, the ability to call the shots."

My throat was dry. "But—that's crazy. Why would anybody do that? An agility trial is never a sure thing. A thousand things can distract a dog and change the outcome. That's what makes it a trial. You can't call an agility trial any more than you can call a—"

"Horse race?" he suggested, and I felt sick.

I grabbed the orange juice and took a swallow. "So what you're saying is that this—this mob person or persons—"

"Organized crime," he corrected.

"Had big money on the outcome of the

Standard Cup—"

"It doesn't have to be just the Standard Cup," he pointed out. "If I know the way these things work, and I do, there has to be more than one commercially sponsored contest, am I right?"

He was right. I tried to stop the big-screen unfurling before my eyes of the names of pet supply companies and big-box pet stores that sponsored competitions. I cleared my throat tightly. "Had big money on the Standard Cup," I repeated, "but they were betting *against* Neil and Flame. All was well until Neil hedged his bets, so to speak, with Bryte."

Miles nodded soberly. "It's never the horse," he said. "It's the jockey. Or, to be precise, it's the combination. They figured Neil for a no-show because of the palimony thing with Marcie. They didn't count on him going all out with his own dog. So, in the end, they made sure he didn't."

Suddenly I was intensely homesick. All I'd ever wanted was a little playtime, a chance to get away, a respite from the challenges of the past year. This was turning into a nightmare, and I wanted to go home. Things were so much simpler in Hansonville. Miles must have seen it in my face because he reached across the table and took my hand.

"I'm so sorry, honey," he said.

I said forlornly, "I really kind of liked Marcie. She raised such great dogs."

Our food arrived, and I asked the waitress to bring my take-out orders now so the food would have a chance to cool before I gave it to the dogs. Miles dug into his plate with gusto, and I picked apart my grilled cheese, nibbling on the French fries.

"What doesn't make sense," Miles said after a time, "is why they would go after Marcie. Breaking Neil's knee is one thing. It's practical and efficient and it solves the problem."

I stared at him, the sandwich motionless a few inches from my mouth. "Who are you?"

He brushed the comment aside absently. "But what they did to Marcie... That's not only killing the golden goose. It's sloppy."

"She must have double-crossed them somehow."

"I don't see how. There wasn't time."

I took a bite of my sandwich, chewing thoughtfully, thinking back over the timeline of events since the trial yesterday. I swallowed hard and reached for my orange juice. I looked at Miles, and slowly it all came together.

"Oh my God, of course," I said. I put my glass down with a thump. "I think I know who did it."

CHAPTER FIFTEEN

Two hours, ten minutes before the shooting

Jeremiah Allen Berman loved the twenty-first century. Everything was so easy these days. He'd been out less than a month and already he'd met three different guys that were living high, hardly lifting a finger. One of them was selling credit card numbers he collected by pointing his cell phone at a gas pump—whoever would've thought of a thing like that?—and another lifted complete IDs from hospital records. The third fellow probably worked the hardest, but he was making a killing backing up his truck beside an eighteen-wheeler in the freight yard, clipping the security cable, and off-loading the contents. With a crew of six, he could be in and out in fifteen minutes and do a half million dollars in merchandise a night. What a world they lived in. It was just made for guys like Jeremiah Allen Berman.

The hard-██████ in prison used to try to rag on him about vo-hab—*try* being the operative word because nobody lasted long on Berman's bad side—but his daddy didn't raise no fool. Daddy used to say, "This world, she's made for the thinking man." Then he'd spit a stream of tobacco juice and let out a screech of laughter that could raise the hairs on a dead man██████and add, "A thinking man that knows how to swing a two-by-four upside somebody's head, am I right, boy?"

Jeremiah Berman slid onto the sticky barstool in front of a big-screen television and grinned to himself. "You don't know how right you were, Daddy," he said. "You just don't know."

He reached for his cell phone and swore when the movement reminded him of the pain in his hand. The ██████ thing was already starting to swell up. He should have shot that ██████████ when he'd had the chance.

The bartender gave him an odd look. "Get you something?"

"Budweiser," he grunted without looking up and carefully plucked out his cell phone with the other hand.

He'd stolen the cell phone, along with a hundred ten dollars cash, from his fourteen-year-old niece, who knew what he'd do to her if she told anybody. Not that she didn't deserve it, anyhow, prancing around the house all dressed up like a twenty-dollar ~~whore~~ on New Year's Eve. And what ~~the hell~~ was his brother thinking, giving her a cell phone that cost more than one of them fancy new flat-screen TVs when he was always groaning about how he could barely make the mortgage and drove a six-year-old pickup? Well, he didn't exactly drive it anymore, since Berman dumped it in the mall for a Honda with a spare key hidden in the wheel well. But still, he deserved what he got. Just how often had that ~~son of a bitch~~ come to see him when he was upstate, anyhow?

On the other hand, the M14 his brother kept locked away in a steel gun cabinet in the basement was a pretty good consolation prize. He could let a lot slide for the satisfaction of knowing that baby was going to be by his side if he needed it.

Nobody messed with Jeremiah Allen Berman. Hadn't he just proven that? It had taken twenty years, but he'd settled the score, fine and good.

The cash was almost gone, but it didn't matter.

He'd get more. Now that he'd taken care of business, he had plenty of schemes. And none of them involved knocking over gas stations for a handful of cash, either. He was smart, now. He was using his head. And those tar-faces up at Marion who used to jeer at him about his computer classes were laughing out the other side of their ▓▓▓▓ now.

There was a computer in every public library. Anybody could just walk in and connect to the Internet. You could sit outside a coffee house or a book store or a hundred other places and nobody would ever know who you were while you stalked them on Facebook, stole their bank account numbers, ripped off their credit cards, sent them threatening e-mails, and one day, maybe even showed up at their door. It was a world wide open. And it was waiting for him.

So he paid for his beer with a twenty, logged into Facebook, and scrolled back through his recent history. There she was outside the Pembroke Host Inn sign in her baseball cap and dog sweatshirt with a big yellow dog at her side, posting, "Ready to take every blue ribbon in Pembroke, SC!" More pictures of the yellow dog, more stupid posts. Some black and white dogs, more posts. There she was in her baseball cap and dog shirt with the black and white dog. More pictures of dogs. More pictures of the hotel. He just smiled.

"Sayonara, baby," he murmured and then he looked up and there she was on the television.

At first he couldn't believe it. The television news had to be wrong. There it said in bold caption over the video of some woman with a dog, talking to a reporter: *Hotel guest Raine Stockton finds body of murdered woman.*

He said hoarsely, "Turn it up."

When the bartender didn't react quickly enough he half lifted himself from the stool and shouted, "I said turn it up, ▓▓▓▓▓."

The bartender took his time pointing the remote control at the television and raising the volume. All he caught was the last part of the segment.

"Thank you, Miss Stockton," the serious-faced reporter said as she turned to the camera. "Once again, police are still investigating this bizarre assault and murder of a hotel guest outside the Pembroke Host Inn here in Pembroke. The identity of the victim is being withheld pending notification of next of kin. We'll keep you updated as the story develops. This is Carolina Mays, WCGA News."

Somebody said, "Thank you, Carolina," as Raine Stockton and her yellow dog moved out of the shot.

Jeremiah Allen Berman stared at the television screen in slack-jawed disbelief for a minute, then became aware of the sharp gaze of the bartender and dropped his eyes to his phone. She was still there, in the baseball cap and the dog shirt. Brown ponytail, slim figure. But there was something different. How could she be different? She'd come out with her black and white dog ten minutes after he'd called her room, hadn't she? *How could she be different?*

He took a long slug of his beer, and his face hardened as he swallowed. Brown ponytail, dog shirt, baseball cap. And behind her, the entrance sign to a fairgrounds. Google maps found it in .03 seconds.

Jeremiah Allen Berman was nobody's fool. Nobody's. And now he was ~~furious.~~

* * *

Detective Laraposa seemed less than excited to learn why I was calling. "You do realize we're investigating a murder here, Ms. Stockton," he said. "So unless you have some new information that pertains to the case…"

"Look," I said, "I don't know how this is connected to Marcie's killer, but you need to have your men search the field behind the hotel for a lead pipe. My dog Cisco found it this morning and he was showing an usual amount of interest in it."

"Ms. Stockton—"

"The kind of interest he usually shows when an article has recent human scent on it, or strong scent, like blood."

"The medical examiner didn't find any sign that the victim was struck with any sort of weapon."

"But her boyfriend was. Neil Kellog."

Now he was interested. "What do you know about that?"

"I just left him. He's co-owner of the dogs and—well, that doesn't matter. The thing is, the way he described the man who attacked him sounded a lot like the man I saw with Marcie yesterday afternoon at the hotel. But what I forgot to tell you was that he was carrying a bag with him when the two of them went to walk the dogs. What if the lead pipe that he used to attack Neil with was in the bag? And what if the reason he took the bag with him when they walked the dogs was to get rid of the weapon in the field, where no one would associate it with the attack on Neil?"

The detective was silent for a moment. Then he

said, "Thank you, Miss Stockton. We'll look into it. We have your contact information if we need anything else."

All in all, that was a very unsatisfactory conversation.

I made a wry face as I tucked the phone back into my pocket. "They'll look into it."

Miles's expression was mostly sympathetic. "Not like working with the hometown cops, huh?"

"I can't believe she sat down at the table with us last night as calm as you please, knowing Neil was passed out on the floor with pain." I gave a dismayed shake of my head. "I thought I was a better judge of character than that."

"Maybe she didn't know," Miles suggested. "Her boyfriend—or whoever it was who was with her—might not have told her. People who take care of problems like that don't usually give the details."

I said, "I'm starting to see where Melanie gets her really, really bad television viewing habits."

He didn't acknowledge that, frowning thoughtfully. "I still don't see how any of it relates to the murder, though."

The waitress brought the take-out boxes and our check. Miles reached for it automatically, checked himself, and passed it to me with a smile. I turned down the corners of my mouth and dug some cash out of my back pocket.

"Where are we going from here?" he asked, making a visible effort to appear cooperative.

"To feed the dogs," I replied. I left cash on the table and gathered up the foam take-out boxes. Miles stood, and I glanced up at him as I slid out of the booth. "And then," I conceded, "back to the hotel to check out. But first we have to go by the fairgrounds and turn the dogs over to Aggie. "

He took the boxes from me. "And after that? I like to plan my day."

I hesitated. I know it sounds crazy, and maybe I was in some kind of shock, but in my heart I was grieving the loss of the three-day trial and perhaps our last chance at a double qualification. Miles must have seen it in my face, because his lips tightened, and I could feel his disappointment in me. I said, "I'll let you know, okay?"

He nodded, but his tone was distant as he said, "Sure." He took out his phone and checked his messages while we walked to the car.

I don't like feeding dogs out of take-out containers—they have a tendency to accidentally eat the containers—so I scrambled around in my dog bag until I came up with two collapsible food bowls and an aluminum water bowl that I always kept in the car for emergencies. I filled the three bowls with steak and eggs and watched the dogs inhale their feasts while Miles walked a few feet away and returned phone calls. I offered each of the dogs a water chaser in their empty bowls and decided to wait until we got to the fairgrounds to walk them. I'd just finished wiping down the empty bowls and putting them away when Miles returned.

He said, "How about dropping me off at the hotel so I can pick up my car? Since you don't know what you want to do yet."

"Oh, for heaven's sake, Miles, don't pout. This isn't the way I wanted to spend my weekend either, you know." I held out my hand for the car keys. "I'll drive."

He tossed the keys to me. "Not pouting. There's still time to drive to the beach if you want to. If not, I'm going back to Atlanta." He got into the passenger seat and closed the door before adding, "As soon as I see you safely checked into another hotel."

I drew a breath for a snippy remark, thought better of it, and started the engine.

We didn't speak again until I stopped in front of the side entrance to the hotel. The scene of the crime, with all its trappings, was on the opposite side of the building, and I'd deliberately avoided going that way. On this side of the building the parking lot was mostly empty, no one was coming or going, and it might have been any ordinary day at any hotel in that quiet space between checkout and check-in times.

Miles put away his phone and looked at me. "Do you want me to pack the rest of your things?"

"My bag's already packed," I admitted and reached to turn off the ignition. "I should go in and get it."

He said, "Go on and take care of the dogs. I'll bring it to the fairgrounds. Maybe by then you will have decided what you want to do."

Why didn't I just tell him I'd go to the beach with him? Was that really such a bad idea? Of course they wouldn't cancel an AKC sanctioned trial with over three hundred entries because of what had happened to Marcie, but did I really think there was any possibility at all of having fun now? Would any of us who had been at the hotel this morning be able to compete with any spirit at all, and would anyone even be able to look at an

222

agility course today without thinking of Neil and Bryte, who wouldn't be running… and who might not, in fact, ever run together again? My boyfriend just offered me a quiet beach to walk on and a strong shoulder to lean on. Of course I should say yes.

I said, "Thanks. I'll meet you at the fairgrounds, then."

A flash of impatience crossed his eyes and he opened the door. Then he hesitated, turned back, and leaned across the seat to brush my cheek with a kiss. He winked at me. "Love you, babe," he said. "It's something people say."

I should have said it back. Later I would die a thousand deaths inside, over and over again, wishing I'd said it back. Instead, I gave him an exasperated look and replied, "I'm not your 'babe.'"

He grinned and got out of the car. "I know," he said.

He closed the door and lifted his hand in a casual wave as he took out his key card. I drove away and didn't look back.

CHAPTER SIXTEEN

One hour, forty minutes before the shooting

Dog Daze Boarding and Training had started its life as the horse barn behind Judge Stockton's big old Colonial farmhouse. Before that, when the house was first built in the 1890s, it housed livestock; the judge had added concrete floors and good ventilation to pamper the riding horses his wife Jessica loved so much. A fire had damaged much of the structure a short time ago, but it had been rebuilt with state-of-the-art concrete kennels that opened onto individual runs, an indoor training room, and an attractive front façade that featured colorful cutouts of playful puppies climbing the walls and jumping over the door frame. Paw prints were stamped into the concrete walkway that led to the front entrance, and Buck followed them inside.

Maude was just coming out of the boarding area, drying her hands on a paper towel, and she looked surprised to see him. "Good day to you, Buck," she said. The pressurized door swung shut on the sound of barking and the faint smell of antiseptic that came from the corridor behind her. "What a lovely surprise. Raine's not here, I'm afraid."

She was a slim, athletic woman in her sixties with short, no-nonsense silver hair and a crisp British accent she sometimes confessed she'd worked hard to keep over the forty years she had lived in Hanover County. She'd been a fixture around the Stockton household for as long as Buck could remember, first as the judge's clerk, then as family friend, and finally as Raine's mentor and business partner. There wasn't much that had gone on in this county over the past forty years that Maude didn't know about, nor were there many questions that she couldn't answer.

He said, "That's okay. Actually, I think you're the one I need to talk to."

On the drive out, he'd tried to erase the anxiety that kept gnawing away at his stomach and furrowing his brow, but the look on Maude's face told him he hadn't quite been successful. She said, "It sounds serious." She tossed the paper towel in the trash. "Come into the office and sit down. What's troubling you?"

"I need some help with an old case of Judge Stockton's." He followed her through the swinging doors that separated the reception area from the playfully decorated yellow and blue office where they kept the records and did the paperwork associated with the business. One of Maude's silky-coated golden retrievers had been napping behind the desk; he rose and stretched as they entered, and Buck held out a hand for him to sniff.

Maude said, "I thought Roe was in charge of cold cases now. Shall I make some tea? Or coffee if you like."

"No, thanks." He scratched the golden retriever behind the ears and was rewarded with a satisfied grin. "And this is one of those cases that has Roe stumped as much as it has me. Probably because there's nothing there. At least I hope there's not."

Maude pulled out a rolling black chair from behind the desk and sat down, gesturing Buck to one of the straight-backed guest chairs opposite. She leaned forward, resting her elbows on her knees. The golden retriever stretched out behind the desk and went to sleep. "I'm intrigued," she said. "What can I do to help?"

Buck unfolded the sheaf of papers in his hand and passed it to her. On top was the ID photo of James Allen Berman. "I was hoping you could give me some inside information on this case from the nineties. Started out as an armed robbery at the Cash-n-Carry, ended up as a murder."

Maude looked at the picture and kept on looking at it. She didn't raise her eyes or make a move or even draw a breath, but Buck didn't think it was his imagination that her lips seemed to lose color. He watched her carefully as he continued.

"Judge Stockton actually proposed the deal that pled it down to second, but he seemed to be worried about this guy. He wanted to keep an eye on him when he got out, but nobody seems to know why."

Still she didn't look up. She was like a statue, frozen there, porcelain white skin, marble white lips, the glossy cap of her hair suddenly looking as cold as marble. And she said nothing.

"So I talked to a fellow who knew Berman while he was upstate. He seemed to think Berman had a grudge against Judge Stockton. Now, a lot of inmates are bitter about the lawman that sent them up, and some of them are even stupid enough to threaten revenge. But I don't think I've ever heard of one who swore to get even with the judge who granted their plea bargain and even went so far as to carry around his obituary like some sort of target or something. The judge died of a stroke. I was here when it happened. Something's missing from this picture, Maude. I was hoping you could help me put it together."

Still, she remained silent. She was silent for so long, so silent and so motionless, that Buck was starting to grow alarmed. Then she said softly, "Twenty years. My word. It goes by so quickly."

She set the papers aside and, without looking at Buck or, in fact, anything else in the room, she rose and walked to the window. She repeated absently, almost to herself, "My word."

The golden retriever, sensing her distress, went to stand beside her. She dropped a hand to his head, stroking it, gazing out the window. "I told him he should recuse himself," she said without turning. She spoke in a leisurely, almost ruminating manner, as though relating a tale that was of only the most passing interest to either of them. "But he was the district court judge. How could he take himself off the case without explaining why? And the explanation would have destroyed Jessica. He couldn't be the cause of that. Neither of us could."

Buck frowned, completely lost now. "Jessica," he repeated, baffled. "Raine's mother—the judge's wife?"

"It was the car, you know. The car that poor boy hit that night, the car that would have proven—or at least cast a reasonable doubt—that he was not at the gas station at the time of the robbery. Don Kramer built his whole case around it. If he could've found the people in that car…"

Buck said uncertainly, "Mrs. Stockton? Was she driving the car he hit that night?"

Maude shook her head slowly and turned. Her smile was tired and infinitely sad. "No," she said. "I was."

The fairgrounds looked different than they had the day before. The RVs were still there with their barking dogs bouncing in their ex-pens and the smells of morning bacon and coffee lingering faintly in the air. The rows of minivans and SUVs were the same, hatchbacks open on crated border collies, cocker spaniels, bearded collies, and shelties. The same colorful blue and yellow agility equipment was set up under the pavilion, and the jumpers-with-weaves course was defined by white gating a few dozen yards away. Dogs were being walked in the grassy area, canvas camp chairs were set up around the ring, and the smell of greasy nachos and roasting hotdogs came from the concession area. But the applause seemed muted, the runners lacked enthusiasm, and the day itself seemed wrapped in a pall of dull-gray light.

By force of habit, I took Cisco's lightweight canvas crate from its storage position behind the front seat and slung its strap over one shoulder, my day bag over the other. Cisco waited patiently—we'd worked hard on that—until I unclipped his seat belt, took his leash in hand, and said, "Release." He bounded out and began to sniff the ground beneath us for familiar footprints.

The border collies poked their noses over the barrier and I knew they needed to be walked. "You're next," I promised them. "I'll be right back."

I couldn't help noticing as I passed the pavilion that there were fewer spectators than there had been yesterday. Some were gathered in small, tense groups, and I knew they were talking about

Marcie. One woman was crying. Others, oblivious to the drama that was taking place beneath the surface, were widely scattered around the bleachers, studying their course maps or watching the competition, some with dogs but most without. I paused to watch a golden retriever fly across the first three jumps of a sequence, and realized it was Gunny when I recognized the handler. I put down my crate and bag and stood to watch.

Gunny knocked a bar and missed two weave poles, but it wasn't a bad run, all things considered. When the ring crew started breaking down the course, I realized with a pang that the next event was the one Cisco and I had entered for the afternoon.

Ginny saw me and waved. I set up Cisco's crate near a concrete pillar while she and her mother made their way over to me with Gunny. There was no point in trying to claim a space in the livestock barn. We wouldn't be here that long.

"Nice run," I told Ginny, because it's something you say even when you know it's not exactly true.

She shrugged. She looked as tired and dispirited as I felt. "My heart wasn't really in it."

Aggie said, "Have you heard anything?"

I tucked my day bag inside the crate and

zipped it up. "I have the border collies with me," I said. "Neil can't take them. He just got out of the hospital."

Their shocked looks didn't surprise me, but it was a long story and I didn't want to stand around while I told it. "The dogs need to be walked. Can you give me a hand?"

Ginny put Gunny in his crate while I got Bryte and Flame out of the car. Ginny took Bryte and Aggie took Flame, and we started across the dog walk field while I explained the events of the morning. My mother always said "evil be to him who evil speaks" so I didn't think it was necessary to include the details—which, to be honest, were mostly fabricated by Miles—about organized crime and mobsters breaking Neil's knee. The point I wanted to make was that Neil was as much of a victim as Marcie and, for the time being at least, he wasn't capable of taking care of the dogs.

"It's like," Aggie said, catching a trembling lip between her teeth, "a conspiracy or something. I never imagined that someone we knew… that something like this could happen to people in our own club…"

Cisco romped at the end of his twenty-foot leash, play-bowing to the border collies, sniffing the grass, trying to tell the world that everything was going to be okay. I couldn't help smiling as I watched him, and I suddenly wished Miles were here.

I said, "Have you heard anything about Marcie's next of kin?"

Ginny said, "She was president of the club, but no one knew her very well." Her tone was subdued. "She had someone working for her, a kennel boy, who took care of the dogs while she was away. She didn't have many real friends. Someone said her mother was in Pennsylvania, and she has a sister somewhere. Neil would know, but I guess he's in no condition to think about it now."

"We'll take the dogs, of course," Aggie assured me. "I'm sure once we get them back home we'll be able to find out who's in charge."

I nodded. "I gave Neil your phone number. He was... well, he wasn't really coping very well. But I know he'll be in touch."

Aggie shook her head solemnly. "Such a horrible thing."

And Ginny pushed her fingers across wet eyes. "Unbelievable," she said thickly. "I really just want to go home."

I helped them load the border collies into the

back of their minivan, and we talked briefly about crates and dog food and all the other things that must have been left in the hotel room and were by now in police custody. It was all so incredibly sad. I looked at Flame, who had fought so valiantly to try to lead us to her mistress, and I leaned through the open window of the hatchback and took her face between my hands. "You are a good, good girl," I told her solemnly. "You did everything right. You did."

I looked at Aggie. "You'll make sure she gets a good home?" I said. "Not just with someone who wants to win, but with someone who wants *her*. Do you promise?"

Aggie smiled at me. "Honey, I'm a dog person. You ask Maude. We know what's important. I'll take care of this little girl, don't you worry about that."

I believed her. And I had to leave it at that.

Cisco and I walked back to the pavilion. The course for the next event was almost complete, and the competitors were starting to gather. I could almost smell their adrenaline, taste their anticipation as they studied the obstacles, visualized their runs, and waited anxiously for the judge to call them in for the briefing. This was the best part. No one was a loser now. Anything was possible. Someone would leave today with the fastest collie in the southeast. Or the fastest golden, or cocker, or bichon. Someone else would break the old record for fastest weaves. Someone would get a double-Q. Someone would be high in trial. Titles would be given out by the dozen. Dogs would go home with squeaky toys and their owners would tack another ribbon on the wall and swell with pride. Years of training would pay off today, or not, dreams would come true, or not, and every competitor here would go home with the best dog in the world. This was why I loved this sport. For this moment.

Cisco made a high sharp sound in his throat and his ears went forward. I shook myself out the reverie of longing to follow his intense gaze, but I really didn't have to wonder what had caught his attention. Sarah was standing on the other side of the ring from us with Brinkley, and Cisco's tail was swinging like a fan on high speed at the sight of him. She was in deep conversation with a man who had his back to us, and as I watched, Brinkley noticed Cisco and gave a sharp bark of greeting. Sarah looked at him and then at us. She waved and then, surprisingly, said something to the man and pointed to me.

He turned and looked straight at me. My heart stopped.

It was the big-shouldered man who'd been with Marcie last night at the hotel. He started walking toward us, and as he did, the gap in his half-zipped windbreaker widened just long enough to reveal the curve of a leather shoulder holster and the unmistakable glint of a gun.

Maude looked at Buck with something almost like sympathy on her face. Sympathy for the blank incomprehension that must have shown in his eyes, or sympathy for what she knew she was about to say would do to him.

She said, "Isn't there a saying about chickens that come home to roost? What are the odds that young man should be tried on a capital offense before the one judge who could have testified to his innocence? Yet, in another way, it was almost inevitable." She smiled vaguely. "You see, men like Jonathan aren't fashioned to be less than honorable. It isn't in their DNA. If they stray, or even try to stray, from that very rigid line that's their truth, it's as though they have an invisible compass that pulls them back, correcting the course. Most of the time that compass is their own conscience. But sometimes it takes the form of the hand of God."

Buck said slowly, "You're saying Judge Stockton was in the car—the one Berman hit that night? But that doesn't make any sense. Why didn't he report the accident? If not that night, then later when he realized the car was material evidence in a case... What was the big deal? Why keep it a secret?"

"He was supposed to be at a conference in Seattle that weekend," she explained simply. Her hands were laced together lightly before her, her shoulders firm and square. The golden retriever, reading something in her posture, sat at her side with shoulders straight and head high, mimicking her stance. "I was supposed to be at a dog show. Instead, we were together at a lodge in the mountains. It wasn't the first time. We were quite, quite desperately in love and had been for years."

It was a long time before Buck could speak, though half-formed thoughts buzzed around and collided in his head like broken-winged insects. He couldn't quite look at her, this woman he thought he knew, had known for all of his life. But he couldn't judge her, either. He wanted to, but he couldn't.

He said after a time, with difficulty, "So he broke the law, lied to two officers of the court, and sent an innocent man to prison to protect you."

She drew in a sharp breath. "Oh dear, no. I wanted to come forward. When I realized—I was the one who recognized Berman when the case came across Jonathon's desk six months later, and when I put the timeline together, I realized he couldn't possibly have been here committing a robbery and sixty miles away on the Centerline Road at the same time. I knew we had to speak up… but by then we couldn't, you see."

Into Buck's stunned and unwelcoming silence she explained gently, "By then, Jessica had been diagnosed with cancer. Jonathon, Raine—they were all she was living for. If the truth had come out, if she'd learned about us, it would've destroyed her. And neither one of us was willing to do that. As much as he loved me, he loved Jessica more. Enough to sacrifice his integrity, his principles, his ethics, and his career for. Enough to lie for. Enough to send a man to prison for a crime he didn't commit."

Buck couldn't remain seated. He stood, paced a few steps across the small room, pushed his hand through his hair. The golden retriever watched him alertly. He drew in a breath and released it in measures. He tried to focus on the pieces that were falling into place. All he could think about was how easy it was to believe what you got used to seeing. All those years, he'd never guessed. No one had.

He said, "Judge Stockton was afraid Berman would recognize him if the case went to trial. That's why he pushed the deal."

"In part," Maude admitted. "In other part—he was afraid Berman would be convicted. It was a death penalty case. He couldn't have lived with that. The young man was no saint, and no doubt he deserved a good deal more than the twenty years he served if all the crimes for which he'd never been convicted were taken into account. But if he'd been convicted of a first-degree murder that he didn't commit… no. Jon couldn't let that happen."

"Then Berman saw the judge's obituary and recognized the photograph." Buck's voice was toneless and his eyes flat. He was thinking aloud. "He put it all together and realized what happened. The judge must've been afraid something like that would happen. That's why he wanted Roe to keep an eye on him."

A slow alarm darkened Maude's eyes.

"Something like what?"

Buck looked at her sharply. "You'd know, wouldn't you, if any strangers had been poking around here the last few weeks? Any strange phone calls Raine might have gotten?"

Maude said, "No, nothing that I know of. Do you think…? Is there cause to be concerned?"

Buck's lips tightened grimly. "Raine needs to know about this," he said. "You handle it any way you want, but she's going to have to know."

Maude's hand fluttered to her throat. "Is she in danger, Buck? Is she in danger because of me?"

"Not now," he said. "Not yet. But twenty years in prison is a long time to hate somebody who did you wrong, and it must've made him even madder when the judge died before he could get out and get even. The obituary would've listed the details about his survivors. That's why he carried it around for so long. That's what he meant by 'sins of the father.' He's a long way from here now, and maybe we'll catch him before he finds Raine, but she'll have to be warned. And sooner or later she'll want to know why."

Maude said softly, "It will break her heart."

For a moment her pain was reflected in Buck's eyes. "I know."

Maude nodded slowly and turned back to the window. "I've a brother in Florida, you know. He's just bought a hotel, and he asked me to consider helping him run it. Perhaps it's time for a change."

Buck knew he should say something, but he didn't know what. In the end, all he could manage was, "You do what you have to do. But tell Raine to give me a call when she gets in, will you?" He started for the door.

Maude said, "That won't be until Sunday."

He looked back her.

"She's at an agility trial in South Carolina," Maude said. "I should think she might've mentioned it to you. It's all she's posted about on Facebook for days. Cisco won a blue ribbon."

Facebook. For some reason that word seemed to echo in his head and along with it a dozen police bulletins he'd received over the past year, all of them jumbled up and unrelated to each other. Everything within him seemed to go cold. He said, "Where in South Carolina?"

"Pembroke. It's the big season opener at the agricultural fairgrounds there. She always—"

Buck snatched out his phone and started dialing, his heart going like a freight train. Maude moved toward him in alarm.

"Buck?"

"~~Damn~~," he said tightly. "Voice mail. ~~Damn~~ it..." He pushed out the door with Maude following helplessly. "Raine, listen to me. You're in danger. Get in your car and drive to the nearest police station, do you hear me? Call me from there. Do it now."

"Buck," Maude called after him. "Is there anything I can do?"

But he was already on another call, lengthening his stride until he was almost running as he moved toward his car. "This is Sheriff Lawson, Hanover County, North Carolina. North Carolina ID NC7548—"

The rest was cut off as he slammed the door of the cruiser and spun the car around in the narrow parking lot. He sped down the driveway, leaving a plume of dust and gravel in his wake, and all Maude could do was watch.

CHAPTER SEVENTEEN

Eight minutes before the shooting

Jeremiah Allen Berman once again admired the wonder of this fine new century into which he had been released: the ease with which people moved to and fro, the determination that allowed them to focus only on themselves and not on what was going on around them. He'd been born for this time. He had.

It had taken him less than an hour to get to the park. No one had stopped him. Why should they? At first he'd worried about how he would transport an assault rifle across an open parking lot and into a pavilion crowded with people, but it turned out to be amazingly simple. This was a dog show. People were carrying all kinds of crazy things — pop-up tents, oversized coolers, foldaway dog houses with air-conditioned fans, roll-up mats, and collapsible canvas chairs. He walked to a vendor's booth, spent twenty dollars on what looked like a yoga mat printed with dog paws, went back to his car, and concealed his weapon inside. The yoga mat had a shoulder strap. No one looked at him twice as he climbed to the very top of the bleachers and settled the mat between his feet, waiting for a certain woman with a brown ponytail in a golden retriever sweatshirt to arrive.

Last night it'd been dark. The mistake was easy to make. But he had over a dozen pictures of her now, scrolling over and over on the wallpaper of his phone. He knew his target. And by now he was just mad enough to enjoy a little collateral damage.

He was calm; he was ready. He didn't break a sweat as he saw her cross into the shadow of the pavilion with the yellow dog. A man was walking toward her. Not a problem. Collateral damage. He began to unwrap his weapon from the paw print mat. No one even glanced his way. His hand where the dog had bitten him hurt like a ~~███████████~~, and his trigger finger was swollen to twice its normal size. That only made him madder. He hoped he'd be able to pick off a few black and white dogs while he was at it.

He slipped down behind the bleacher seat in sniper position. He lifted the rifle, sited his target, and waited for his shot.

I reached automatically into my pocket for my phone and remembered too late it was tucked inside my day bag, which was secured inside Cisco's crate, because that was what I always did with my valuables at a trial. The big-shouldered man kept coming toward me, mouth grim, eyes cold. My hand tightened on the leash and I glanced around a little frantically, but where could I go and what would I do when I got there? There were people everywhere, setting up the course, watching from the stands, gathering in groups outside the ring. Surely I was safer here in front of all these witnesses than anywhere else, and besides, what could he possibly do to me? Then I remembered Neil's knee and one swing of a lead pipe from those powerful arms, and I took an involuntary step backward.

He was upon me.

"Raine Stockton?" he said.

He reached inside his jacket and I drew a breath to scream, but suddenly Cisco gave a happy bark and lunged forward to the end of the leash, sending me stumbling after him. At first I thought my brave dog was protecting me, but then I saw Sarah and Brinkley cross the pavilion toward the practice jump, and Cisco's gaze was rapt upon them. I burst out, "~~██████~~, Cisco!" and then I realized the man hadn't pulled out a gun, but an ID wallet.

He said, "I'm Special Agent Seth Ledbetter, with the State Bureau of Investigation. I wonder if I could talk to you for a minute."

I stared at him. More importantly, I stared at the badge and the photograph ID inside the wallet. I'd seen enough law enforcement badges to know this one was authentic. Nonetheless, I said, "No, you're not. You were with Marcie yesterday at the hotel. I saw you." Cisco barked again and I said sharply, "Cisco, sit!" He complied automatically, but his attention was on the opposite side of the ring and he licked his lips anxiously. I ignored him and looked back at the man opposite me suspiciously. "How did you find me?"

He put away his ID. "I spoke with the detective on the case, who told me you found Marcie Wilbanks's body. And the gentleman at the hotel, Mr. Young, told me you were here."

I knew if I checked my messages I'd find one

from Miles. Still, I was cautious. "What were you doing with Marcie yesterday?"

An expression of such raw grief and regret crossed his eyes that I knew that whatever he said next would be nothing but the truth. He frowned a little, as though in attempt to hide the emotion, and his lips tightened. "I've been trying to bust a loan sharking ring for over a year now, and Marcie—Ms. Wilbanks—offered to help us set a trap. Over time... we probably became closer than we should have. Yesterday... we were within hours of closing in on them, and the stress was getting to her. No one expected her ex to throw a monkey wrench into the plans with the dogs, and she was upset."

My head was spinning. "Wait a minute. Marcie was working with you? She wasn't in debt to loan sharks and she wasn't trying to fix the Standard Cup?"

He said, "It was a setup. We were trying to get the guys to tip their hand by actually extorting money from her. We didn't count on them going after Kellog, but when they did... we rounded up every one of them within hours."

My mind was busy trying to rearrange the puzzle pieces that had once fit together so well into an entirely different picture. I wasn't having much luck. "But I don't understand. I saw Marcie at dinner last night. I could swear she didn't know anything about Neil being attacked, and she was as nervous as a cat."

He nodded. "She knew it was coming to a head this weekend. We both did. But we didn't learn they'd moved in on Kellog until the police were called after the attack. The hit man still had the bloody tire tool in his car."

"Tire tool?" I repeated. "Not a lead pipe?" Was it possible Cisco had uncovered nothing of more significance than an old piece of construction debris? I'd been wrong about everything else; it hardly seemed far-fetched that I'd been wrong about this too.

He said, "I called Marcie to let her know it was all over about nine last night, and…" He shifted his gaze away, but not before I saw the jagged scar of pain there. "That was the last time I spoke to her."

I said slowly, "But… if you arrested everyone who was involved in the scam, who killed Marcie?"

He said, "That's what I was hoping you could help me figure out." He gestured toward the bleachers. "Could we sit down? I know you've already gone over this with the police, but if you could tell me again everything that happened from the time you got back to the hotel last night until you found her this morning, maybe…"

The ring steward called, "Standard Open! Judge's briefing in five minutes!"

Everyone started moving, hurrying to crate their dogs, put away their course maps, double-knot their shoelaces, pull back their hair, and reassemble in the ring. I felt a pang of jealousy. I'm ashamed of it, but I really did. *One more run…*

And then I saw Miles, leaning with one shoulder against the pillar where Cisco's crate was set up, his hands stuffed into the pockets of his navy windbreaker, Atlanta Braves cap shading his eyes, waiting. How much of his time had been spent waiting for me since we'd met? And how much longer could I reasonably expect him to continue to wait?

I said, "Um, sure. Just a minute, though, okay? I need to put my dog away."

I said, "Cisco, with me." And we started toward Miles.

We'd gone less than a dozen steps when the inevitable happened. Brinkley sailed over the practice jump, made a perfect loop to return to Sarah, and Cisco thought it would be a great idea to join him. Completely forgetting about the leash that connected me to him, he spun around and lunged toward the practice jump and his best friend, jerking me completely off course and very nearly off my feet.

That was probably what saved my life, because it was at that very moment that the ground exploded in a pop of dust less than six inches from where I was standing.

People say at first you don't know what's happening. I've been around gunfire all my life and there was a part of my brain that knew *exactly* what was happening. And there was a part of my brain that was saying, *No, no, not here, it can't be,* while yet another part registered screaming and running and people falling on the ground. Milliseconds, only milliseconds passed while dirt exploded all around me and people fell and dogs barked and legs ran and voices screamed. Agent Ledbetter reached for his gun but spun to the ground before he could draw it. Somewhere close a siren screeched and then another. I heard a name—my name—and suddenly Miles barreled into me, not just pushing me, but *throwing* me toward the shelter of the bleachers with such force that I thudded into a support post and lost my breath. I lay gasping like a beached whale and everything was in slow motion, slow desperate motion because Cisco was no longer with me. His leash had been torn from my hand and now I could see him standing in the middle of the pavilion looking confused and uncertain, looking for me. Inside, I screamed, *Cisco!* But I had no breath to make words. Miles pushed away from me and rushed toward Cisco.

He went down in a rain of gunfire, and that was when I found the breath to scream, "*Noooo!*"

But it was too late.

CHAPTER EIGHTEEN

The Aftermath

I remember the wail of sirens was like the howl of coyotes, drawing closer and closer and louder and louder in those endless seconds of death-quiet before the world started spinning again. Suddenly no more gunfire. Suddenly only broken sobs in the stillness, the thin high bark of a small-breed dog. The smell of cordite and dust and spicy nachos. The drone of a distant RV generator. And then somewhere above my head was a sharp command that had the word "Secure!" in it. I remember that, even though before it was spoken I was already half-running, half-crawling, stumbling and falling, heaving great big choking, horrified gasping breaths, and then I was in Miles's arms.

I remember that it was like being squeezed by a boulder. I remember the taste of his jacket and the salt of my own tears in my mouth, the rock-hard pressure of his chest and arms, and whispers in my ear, something like, "It's okay, baby. It's okay. It is." And Cisco, my big golden guy, worming his way between us, his hot breath on my face, his thick silky fur clasped in my fist. The sound of my ragged breath filled my ears. My face, slick with mucous and tears and mud, pressed first against Cisco's fur and then against Miles's chest. My throat was thick with sobs and I clung to them both, hard. I banged one fist feebly against Miles's chest.

"You went back for him, you idiot." The words were a muffled string of slobber and sobs. "You went back for my dog. You saved him. You went back for my dog."

"Of course I did. Why wouldn't I?"

"You scared me so much! You idiot!" I tried to hit his chest again, but my fist went flat against it, pressing deep into his heartbeat instead. "You scared me so much."

I felt his fingers threading through my hair, cupping my scalp. His voice was husky. "Now you know the feeling."

"It's not just something people say," I whispered wetly. "It's not!"

Miles took my face in his hands and he kissed me, there in the dust in the middle of an AKC trial, mud, mucous, tears, and all, and he said, "I know."

I clung to them, the two guys I loved, until the noise and the shuddering and the terror subsided. We were okay.

We were all okay.

Four people were taken to the hospital, most with minor injuries from falls or shrapnel. A bullet had grazed Agent Ledbetter's shoulder, but he considered the injury minor and was back on the scene with his arm in a dark sling long before the questioning of the witnesses was complete. No dogs were hurt, although some escaped their handlers and were so agitated it took hours to find them. The timely intervention of the SWAT team, who were on site only minutes after Berman arrived, could be thanked for the lack of significant casualties. And, though it was never widely known outside the law enforcement community, Sheriff

Buck Lawson of Hanover County, North Carolina, could be thanked for alerting local authorities to the likely whereabouts and intentions of the perpetrator.

Jeremiah Allen Berman was taken down by a single bullet to the head seventeen seconds after his shooting rampage began. It seemed much longer than that.

"The browser history on his stolen cell phone showed he'd been stalking you for weeks," Agent Ledbetter explained. He'd been our liaison for information, keeping Miles and Cisco and me separated from the others while still making sure we were informed. "Probably since he got out of prison. You've had links to this dog show on your website since February, and it was easy to track your movements on Facebook."

Though the April afternoon was at least as mild as it had been yesterday, it was cold in the shadows where we sat on the bleachers, or at least it seemed so to me. Even with the jacket Miles had draped over my shoulders and the paper cup of coffee that warmed my hands, even with the gentle happy heat of the golden retriever who pressed against my legs, I couldn't stop the occasional shiver.

"Berman acquired some basic computer skills

in prison," Ledbetter went on, "and probably picked up the rest while he was living with his brother in Georgia. The phone belonged to his fourteen-year-old niece. But there's no doubt he'd been planning this for a long time."

I had managed to get a call through to Buck. He explained that Berman had sworn vengeance on my father, who was the judge who sent him to prison, but he'd been annoyingly vague on the details. I supposed he was right—details didn't matter. What mattered was that no one had been seriously hurt, and Berman would never threaten anyone else again.

Miles said, "So it was Berman who tried to get Raine to leave her room last night?"

Ledbetter nodded somberly. "Most likely. One of the hotel guests was able to identify him as the man who tried to get her to let him into the building yesterday, as well."

"Sarah," I said softly, repressing a shudder. "She was so lucky he didn't hurt her."

"There were quite a few people around yesterday evening, and he probably wasn't willing to take that chance. If he could've gotten her alone inside the building, though, it might have been another story."

His face tightened, though whether the white lines that appeared around his lips were from the pain associated with his wound or from the memory of Marcie, I couldn't tell. "Apparently," he went on, "Marcie left her room to walk her dog shortly after Berman called your room last night. We're still matching DNA, but I suspect it will show it was Berman who attacked her. He had a picture of you on his phone with Marcie's dog, and she was wearing a sweatshirt and baseball cap just like yours. In the dark, he may have mistaken her for you."

I closed my eyes and had to take long, deep breaths to keep down the bitter gorge that wanted to rise in my throat. Miles's arm went around my shoulders.

"He had a dog bite on his hand," Agent Ledbetter added. When I opened my eyes, I saw the faintest ghost of a wan smile touch his lips. "It's likely that might have affected his aim. The dog might not have been able to save her mistress, but who knows how many other lives she saved today."

I entwined my fingers in Cisco's fur, leaned my head into Miles's shoulder, and tried very hard not to cry.

* * *

"Thank God," Wyn kept saying. "Thank God no one was killed. Do you know how many of these things *don't* end that way? Just… thank God you were able to get the police there in time." She reached across and squeezed Buck's hand.

They sat on the small deck Buck had constructed on the back of his house, sipping beers and watching the sun go down over the treetops. Soon he would fire up the grill and take some steaks out of the fridge, but not yet. For the moment, he just wanted to be still and be with her, and be glad that this time, this time everything had turned out all right.

He had turned off the television news and the computer and put his phone on "emergency only." He had talked to Raine, he had talked to Roe; he'd talked to Maude and the Pembroke police chief and the SBI. His office had been giving him updates by the minute. But it was over. For now, at least, it could just be over.

He said quietly, "I still can't get over Judge

Stockton. I don't think I ever will."

She looked at him with sympathy and with a gentle wisdom beyond her years. "The things that a man—or a woman—will do for love don't have to make sense. In fact, they shouldn't."

Buck cast her a sharp and argumentative look, but she stopped him with a shake of her head. "It wasn't Maude he did it for," she said. "That's what you've got to understand. It was his wife, and Raine. Those were the great loves of his life, and even from beyond the grave he tried to protect them. I hope someone takes the trouble to explain it to Raine that way."

After a moment, he smiled at her. "I'll make sure somebody does."

She sipped her beer. "You know," she said, gazing at the sunset, "Roe was there when it happened. If he'd asked the right questions all those years ago, all of this might have been prevented. But he didn't." She looked across at Buck. "You did. You figured it out."

He lifted his beer bottle in a toast to her. "I had a little help."

She inclined her head in acknowledgment and shared the toast to herself. "Damn straight."

He just watched her, smiling. "Which reminds

me, I have something for you. A couple of things, actually."

He reached into his pocket and brought out a folded sheaf of papers. She took them curiously and her face lit up with relief as she read the first one. "Your filing papers. You've decided to run for reelection." She pressed the papers to her heart for one brief, passionate moment, like a hug. "You're doing the right thing, Buck. The *only* thing, for you, this county, everyone. I'm so proud of you!" She leaned forward to kiss him, but he held up a staying hand.

"There's a condition," he said. "Look at the next one."

She shuffled the papers until she came to the next set. She murmured aloud, without looking up, "Application for employment, Hanover County Sheriff's Department."

Buck said, "I have a feeling you'll get the job."

She looked up at him with a gathering storm of mixed emotions in her eyes, but he spoke over her. "I need you, Wyn," he said firmly. "The department needs you. The county needs you. ~~Maybe~~ the biggest mistake I made when I took over was accepting your resignation. Come back. Let's do what we do best together."

Her brow knitted, a dozen conflicting emotions skewed her face. She dropped her eyes to the papers and lifted them again, helplessly, to Buck. "I don't know," she said. "I want to, of course, but politically... Buck, this could be suicide. Everyone knows about us. And if you hire me back, it would be like slapping them in the face with it. All you need is one right-wing bigmouth, not to mention the whole issue of nepotism, and not to mention how it would complicate our personal lives..."

He nodded thoughtfully. "You're right. And if there's one thing I can't stand, it's complications."

He reached again into his pocket and felt two objects there. One was a house key, and the other was a ring. Slowly, and with deliberation, he hooked his pinky around the ring. "So I was wondering," he said, and he brought out the ring, "what you'd think about getting married?"

The police kept everyone in the pavilion, compiling a witness list and taking statements, until close to dark. When they finally told us we could go, there was an odd kind of reluctance to leave, for even though we were bound by tragedy, we were all nonetheless bound. Cisco said good-bye to Brinkley, and I hugged Sarah even though I couldn't quite bring myself to meet her eyes. I was glad, for their sakes, that Ginny and Aggie had left with Gunny and the border collies before the drama began, but I felt a real pang of sorrow that I might never see them again. In only a matter of hours these people, and dogs, had come to mean so much to me. At the same time, I knew the pain of seeing them again and remembering what had happened here wasn't something I ever wanted to experience.

Miles packed up Cisco's crate and supplies in the back of my SUV while I said my good-byes and then came back to walk us to the parking lot. A bluish twilight was starting to fall over the South Carolina countryside, and the busy agricultural fairgrounds, which only yesterday had been the site of such joy and colorful activity, seemed bleak and haunted. Some men were loading the blue and yellow panels of the A-frame into a step van, and a lone RV pulled away toward the exit. A car door slammed in the distance. Except for the police vehicles that were parked close to the pavilion, there weren't more than half a dozen cars left.

Cisco walked in close heel at my side. After the events of the afternoon, he'd been very, very careful to keep his attention focused on me. I had so much to apologize to my dog for. He hadn't bargained on this. I'd promised him a fun weekend. He'd promised to do his best. He had kept his promise. I had not.

Miles held my hand. After a time, I glanced at him uncertainly. "Are you mad at me?"

He looked surprised. "For what?"

"For putting you in danger. And me. And everyone. I was worried maybe you wouldn't want me to hang out with Mel anymore." And before he could answer, I burst out, "I don't know why these things happen to me, Miles, I really don't. I don't mean for them to. But you're right. I lead a reckless, dangerous lifestyle, and I'm always getting into trouble, and I should've gone to the beach with you when you asked. I'm so sorry."

He stepped in front of me, halting my forward progress, and dropped both hands onto my shoulders. Cisco obediently and alertly sat at my side when I stopped. Miles said, "Are you serious?" There was a puzzled, genuinely incredulous frown on his face. "Honey, what happened today wasn't your fault. It was the fault of a crazy man. Even the police, with inside information and advance warning, couldn't stop it. How were you supposed to?"

"That's not the point."

"It's absolutely the point. And another thing. These things keep happening to you because you're bright and curious and stubborn and brave and you have a heart as big as a golden retriever's." The smile in his eyes coaxed a small, reciprocal one from me. "And I would be proud to have Melanie grow up to be just like you. Only…" He fell into step beside me again, dropping one arm to my waist. "Let's not take her to any dog shows for a while."

"Trials," I corrected him. "They're called trials."

He dropped a kiss on my hair. "I love you, babe."

I said, "I love you back." I pressed my head briefly against his shoulder and added softly, "Let's go home, okay?"

So we did.

When we got there, a long and complicated story of love, lies, and betrayal was waiting for me, and it was good to have a friend by my side while I heard it. When that story was finished, I would never look at my life, or the people I loved, in quite the same way again.

Perhaps, after all, that wasn't such a bad thing.

ALL THAT GLITTERS

A Raine Stockton Dog Mystery Bonus Short Story

There are people, I know, who say dogs don't understand Christmas. These people clearly have never had dogs. These same people say dogs have little, if any, long term memory and no ability to conceptualize or categorize events. I would very much like those people to explain to me how a field-champion golden retriever can sit by his handler's side and watch four different birds be shot down and fall in four different places in a marsh six hundred yards away and then, on command, go directly to each bird and return it to the handler—in the precise order that it fell. And then they can explain why my golden retriever, upon seeing a certain green felt wreath wrapped in plaid ribbon come out of its box for the first time every year, automatically sits and starts licking his chops in anticipation.

The Dog Bone Wreath is a Christmas tradition that has gone on as long as I've owned dogs. Every year on December fifteenth, the wreath comes out and is decorated with colorful frosted bone-shaped dog biscuits and hung in a prominent place in the training room. Each day until Christmas, the dogs get a bone from the wreath, like a doggie Advent calendar. Since the wreath is only up ten days a year, and since a year is a really, really long time for a dog, you'd think they would forget in between Christmases. But they never do.

Dogs might not understand the concept of Christmas, but they've never misunderstood the concept of treats.

This year my young friend Melanie—age ten, going on thirty—was helping me decorate the kennel for the Dog Daze annual Christmas party. Her puppy, Pepper, was in the back, having a shampoo and blowout for the big event, and the rest of dogs were out in the play yard with one of the kennel staff. But Cisco refused to be distracted from the excitement he could literally smell on the air. He was Cisco, after all, and tracking was his specialty.

Melanie laughed when the Dog Bone Wreath went up on its hook and Cisco, with the instincts of a born chow-hound, looked up from the cardboard wrapping paper tube he was chewing, spotted the wreath without hesitation, galloped across the room, and skidded to a perfect sit beneath it. Even I couldn't prevent a grin and a respectful round of applause.

"Can he have a biscuit now, Raine?" Melanie asked. "This is day one, right? I think he should have a biscuit now."

It had taken the two of us half an hour to tie the dozens of dog biscuits to the wreath with decorative plaid bows, and we'd enjoyed the display for less than a minute, but what kind of Scrooge would I be to say no? I untied a treat and gave Melanie the privilege of dispensing it.

"Come on," I said, picking up the box of Christmas ornaments. "Everyone's going to be here at two, and we've got to finish decorating the dog tree. Grab that box of Christmas stockings too, will you?"

Melanie plopped her "Santa's Helper" elf hat back atop her unruly dark curls, gave me a snappy salute, and picked up the box of miniature felt stockings that we would be stuffing with dog biscuits as party favors. Cisco made a quick detour to grab his half-chewed cardboard wrapping paper tube and dashed after us.

In a small town like our Smoky Mountain community of Hansonville, North Carolina, December is filled with parties, tree-lightings, pageants, and concerts. I'm happy to say the Dog Daze Christmas party is among the most prestigious of all the community events—at least with the dog crowd. It started out as a way for my business partner, Maude, and me to thank our clients for their patronage throughout the year, but had grown to include just about everyone in town with a dog. We had obedience and agility demonstrations; dog games and human games; cookies, cupcakes, and punch for the humans; and dog biscuits and fresh water for the canines. Everyone brought a wrapped dog toy for the gift exchange and an item from the local shelter's wishlist, which we collected in a big basket by the door and delivered to the shelter after the party. We opened up the play yard and let the dogs run and jump and tumble the way God intended, and, as a happy bonus, we usually signed up a handful of new clients for obedience, grooming, or boarding at the end of the day. It really was my favorite party of the year.

I kept the training room comfortably cool for the dogs, but as we left it for the gaily decorated entry foyer, a rush of warm air, holiday music, and the scent of a very expensive cinnamon and clove kennel deodorizer greeted us. Dog bone-studded garland wrapped in twinkling lights wreathed the room, and a fragrant spruce tree, also twinkling with lights, sat on an elevated table in a corner of the room. Where dogs are involved, it's never a good idea to put the Christmas tree on the floor.

Two long folding tables, decorated with plastic red-and-white paw print tablecloths, were laden with platters of dog biscuits and human cookies, all clearly labeled to avoid misunderstanding. Gingerbread cookies shaped like dog biscuits are a great addition to any dog-themed Christmas party… except when the dog biscuits are also decorated to look like gingerbread men. There was a basket of festive holiday bandannas for our canine guests and a bowl of fruit punch for our human guests, and the centerpiece was a miniature plastic Christmas tree decorated with photographs of all our obedience school graduates for the year. After the party, the proud parents would take their pup's picture home as a memento.

I held the door open with my hip for Cisco, who looked stylish in his own bright green "Santa's Helper" bandanna. Naturally, he was stopped short when the two ends of the long cardboard tube he carried in his mouth wouldn't fit through the door, but he solved the problem by neatly snapping the tube in two with his teeth, picking up both pieces, and prancing through the door with his golden tail waving proudly.

"Hey, look at all this cool dog stuff," Melanie said as I set the ornament box on the floor. She held up a box of silver paw print ornaments and giggled when she found a golden retriever with a pair of wings and a halo. "Is this Cisco?"

"Hardly." I relieved Cisco of the cardboard tube and stuffed it in the trash. Before I could turn around, he'd snatched a cookie from the tray on the table, swallowed it, and was sitting innocently by Melanie's side with nothing but a few multi-colored sugar sprinkles on his muzzle to testify to his crime. It's pointless to correct a dog for his misbehavior after he's consumed the evidence, particularly when there aren't even any witnesses to the crime—so all I could do was scowl meaningfully at Cisco and push the cookie tray away from the edge of the table. "Is there one with horns and a pointy tail?"

"Cisco's a good dog," Melanie corrected me pompously, giving Cisco a scratch behind the ears before stretching to hang the golden retriever angel on the tree. "You just don't appreciate him. Right, Cisco?"

It was Christmas, and I was in a good mood, so I didn't remind Melanie that this morning alone Cisco had overturned the Christmas tree while dashing to the door to greet her when she arrived, left muddy paw prints on her dad's cashmere coat, jumped on the kitchen counter and consumed half a bowl of frosting before I could stop him, and hopelessly shredded the brand new roll of wrapping paper that used to be on the cardboard tube he'd just finished mangling. Granted, that last one was my fault. I should have been watching him.

"I appreciate him plenty," I told Melanie. "But I can appreciate him just as much while he's having a nice timeout in the kennel."

Cisco gave a little woof of protest and dug into the ornament box, coming up with a hand-knitted sheep given to me by my aunt. Melanie laughed.

"See?" she said. "He's trying to help. What would you do without him?"

I gently pried the delicate work of art out of his mouth, blotted off the saliva, and hung it on the tree next to a matching knitted collie, well out of his reach. Cisco dived into the box to see what else he could find and, naturally, turned the box over. He backed up quickly as all the ornaments spilled out around his feet, looking up at me in such consternation that I had to grin. "Life would definitely be a lot less interesting," I admitted, scooping the spilled ornaments back into the box before they were crushed by clumsy paws. "But, you know, if it had been up to me, I never would have gotten him."

Melanie looked surprised. "Really? You didn't want Cisco?"

I felt a ridiculous urge to cover Cisco's ears when she said that, but in typical golden retriever fashion, he'd already lost interest in the Christmas tree and was once again eyeing the buffet table. I gave him a warning, "Ank!" and he quickly returned his attention to me, tail waving innocently. "I didn't know he was Cisco then," I explained to Melanie. "I just didn't think I was ready for a puppy."

"Wow," she said, carefully hanging a row of border collies in tartan plaid bows around the circumference of the tree. "What if you hadn't gotten Cisco? It would be just like that old black-and-white movie Dad made me watch the other night."

For a moment I was baffled, and then I said, "*It's a Wonderful Life*?"

Melanie nodded enthusiastically. "Just think how many people he's rescued," Melanie said, "tracking them down out there in the wilderness. And the bad guys he's put in jail. And what about all the old people he visits in the nursing home and kids in the hospital?"

"Cisco knows what a great dog he is," I said, rescuing a bone-shaped ornament from Cisco's mouth and giving him a little nudge with my knee. "He doesn't need a press agent."

"How many lives do you think he's saved, anyway?"

When Cisco was relaxing at home, as now, it might be hard to convince a stranger that he was a valuable working dog. But when Melanie put it like that, I felt a surge of pride and affection that momentarily overcame my impulse to put Cisco in a permanent down-stay. "A lot," I admitted.

"More than ten?"

"Sure."

"More than twenty?"

I paused to give my guy a scratch under the chin, smiling at him. He reciprocated with a happy swipe of his tongue aimed at my face. "Probably," I agreed, and I thought that in some ways, the most important life he'd saved was my own.

"Of course," Melanie observed confidently, "that's nothing to what my Pepper is going to do when she grows up."

I reached for another ornament. "I wouldn't be a bit surprised."

"We're going to join the FBI and chase down terrorists and spies all over the world. Istanbul, Dubai, Hong Kong, Milan, Paris..."

"The FBI can only chase down terrorists and spies on US soil," I pointed out, suppressing a grin. Her recitation of exotic locales was more suggestive of a series of fashion shows than an international terrorism ring, but I supposed anything was possible.

"Plenty of time for that to change before we join the force," she assured me airily. "The point is, we're going to be real crime-solving heroes, just like you and Cisco."

Of course it was flattering to be thought of as a hero by anyone, but I made a face, keeping a wary eye on my dog as he strolled casually toward the buffet table once again. "There've been a lot of days when 'hero' isn't the first word I thought of to describe Cisco." Then, sharply, I called, "Cisco, here."

Cisco turned guiltily and came back to me, breaking into a heart-melting grin halfway across the room. But I refused to be melted. "Go to your place," I told him sternly, pointing to a yellow mat by the door. His tail dropped a few inches at the words, and he looked over his shoulder toward the mat. Then he spotted the chew bone he'd left there and bounded over to it happily, plopping down on the mat and taking up his bone.

"Say, is this Cisco's baby picture?" Melanie held up a Christmas ornament with a photograph of a golden retriever puppy in a red jingle bell collar sitting on Santa's knee. I couldn't prevent a sentimental smile as I reached for it.

"Yes, it is," I said. "He was eight weeks old. I'd only had Cisco for a few minutes when this was taken. And right after that..." I stretched as high as I could, placing the ornament on a safe, sturdy branch. "Cisco solved his first crime."

"Really?" Her eyes lit with the avid interest of someone who watched far too many cop shows on television, in my opinion. "Who'd he nab? A kidnapper? Gangbanger? A cold-blooded serial killer? Maybe he busted up a whole drug cartel!"

The corners of my lips twitched as I glanced across the room at Cisco, who held the bone between his two front paws and was contentedly munching away. "Much bigger than that," I assured her. "As a matter of fact," I added, and I felt a twinkle come into my eyes as I pulled out another handful of ornaments and looked back at her, "it's really kind of an interesting story…"

It hadn't been a good year for me, nor for the majority of the county. The textile plant that had provided jobs for almost half the families in the county had closed down, which drastically affected the economy of our small, isolated mountain town. Shops and businesses were starting to cut back their hours, which is never a good sign, and according to Aunt Mart, who was in charge of just about every charitable organization in town, donations to the Charity Drive were down while requests for charity had never been higher. According to Uncle Roe, who was married to Aunt Mart and who also happened to be the sheriff of Hanover County, crime was also up. That surprised no one but Aunt Mart, who liked to see the best in everyone.

I probably should have been more concerned about the unemployment rate, the rising crime, and the general state of need surrounding me, but as I said, I hadn't had a good year, either. This would be my first Christmas without my father, who died of a stroke earlier that year. I was recently separated—for the second time—from the man to whom I'd been married for ten years, and who'd been my best friend since high school. I was still at the stage where I kept expecting to hear his footsteps in the hallway, and I picked up the phone to call him several times a day before I remembered we didn't do that anymore. ~~That sucked~~.

And, perhaps most devastatingly, my golden retriever Cassidy had died at age thirteen that summer. She was the one who taught me everything I know about dogs. She was the first certified search and rescue dog in Hanover County, and her find rate was ninety-eight percent. She made me look like a superstar. She had more awards than a Nobel laureate and more letters after her name than an Oxford professor. But at the end of the day, she was the one who curled up on the sofa beside me and shared the popcorn on movie night, who was waiting at the door every time I picked up my car keys, who laid her head upon my knee when I was sad, and who danced with excitement when I was happy. She made me who I was. Now she was gone, and I was alone.

And, almost to add insult to injury, it now appeared as though I would lose my job, too. I stared in disbelief at the letter that had arrived in the morning mail. *Due to cutbacks in federal funding, we've been forced to downsize…*

I'd worked for the Forest Service here in the Smoky Mountains since college. It was all I'd ever wanted to do. I wasn't sure I really even knew how to do anything else.

From my supervisor Rick, who graduated two years ahead of me in high school, was a scrawled note on the bottom of the official letter.

Raine, call me. We'll work something out.

Great. The man had graduated ninety-sixth out of a class of one hundred two, and now I was depending on him to "work something out." Terrific.

Donna Ball

"Merry Christmas to me," I muttered. I flung my booted feet atop the kitchen table and dropped my head back onto the chair. And there was absolutely no one to tell me not to do it. That made me even more depressed.

When the phone rang, I almost didn't answer it. Given the way my luck was running, it had to be more bad news. I answered it curtly, "Raine Stockton."

"Hey, Raine," said the chirpy voice on the other end of the line. "This is Rose down at dispatch. We've got a call about an abandoned dog out on Mockingbird Place, and your uncle wanted to know wouldn't you mind going out there to check it out. The boys are just covered up with work down here, and the sheriff said to be sure and tell you he'd really appreciate it."

Our small county couldn't afford an animal control officer, so when a complaint about a dog came in it was usually through the sheriff's office. Unless it was a dog bite case; most of those calls were referred to the Humane Society. And since I'd been president of the Humane Society for the past four years, that meant me. With a longsuffering sigh, I copied down the address, pulled on my coat, and went out into the cold to Mockingbird Place.

The address led me to a row of small square houses a few blocks from the center of town. Fifty years ago they'd probably been perfectly respectable middle income homes; now they were a couple of notches below that. Most of them had the not-quite-neglected look of rental property, with shabby lawns and worn shingles. I pulled into the short dirt driveway of a pale yellow clapboard house with a mud-stained cement block foundation, and I saw the dog immediately. A sable and white collie of about a year old sat imperiously atop a dog house inside a 10x10 chain link enclosure. At least I thought it was a collie. Her coat was so muddied and matted with neglect it was difficult to tell. She didn't bark when I got out of the car; she didn't jump down and rush the fence to greet me. She just sat atop the dog house with all the composure of a royal princess and watched as I approached.

"Well, hello there, Your Majesty," I said softly, putting my hand on the latch of the gate to the dog's enclosure. "Do you mind if I come in?"

The screen door of the house next door slammed, and a woman came down the steps, hugging a pink cardigan to her. "Hello!" she called. "Hello, are you here about the dog?"

I admitted I was and she introduced herself. "I hated to call," she said, "but the family left last week. She said the propane tank was dry and they didn't have any heat—a sweet young thing with three children under school age, her husband left last month, the no-account so-and-so, and she's been doing the best she can since then, I guess. She and the children went to her sister's, but she couldn't take the dog, so I've been feeding it and making sure it had water, but the bag of food she left is almost gone and it's supposed to get down in the teens tonight. She didn't leave me a way to call, and I'd just hate to see the poor thing freeze to death. It's a sweet dog."

I assured her that she'd done the right thing and entered the pen with a slice of hot dog in one hand and a slip leash in the other. The collie didn't fuss as I dropped the leash over her head, and she nibbled on the hot dog I offered her with a delicacy that suggested she was simply being polite.

"We'll take her to the vet to make sure she's up on her shots," I told the neighbor, "and board her until the owner claims her. But if she isn't claimed in five days, we put her up for adoption. I'll leave you one of my cards and slip another one under the front door so the owner can call when she comes back."

The neighbor took my card, but shook her head sadly, hugging the pink sweater closer to her. "She won't come back. And even if she does, she won't call you. She can barely take care of those children, much less a dog."

I suspected she was right, but it wasn't my job to say so. The collie hopped into the back of my SUV and walked nicely into the wire crate I'd prepared for her. I was just locking her in when I heard the sound of a big truck coming around the bend. It was a propane tanker, and to my surprise, it pulled into the driveway beside my car. The driver got out and came around to me. "Miz Chambliss?"

"No," I said, shaking my head. "I'm just here to—"

"She's not here," the neighbor said, coming over to us. The engine of the propane truck rumbled in the background and she raised her voice to be heard. "It got too cold when they ran out of gas."

"Well, this ought to help." He went around the side of the truck and started uncoiling the filler hose. "We got an order to fill the tank this morning, along with three hundred dollars in cash to cover it. Somebody left it in the drop box last night, along with this note." He reached in the pocket of his flannel shirt and pulled out a torn half-sheet of white paper. On it was scrawled, "From your Secret Santa."

I lifted an eyebrow and smiled at the neighbor. "Well, that's good news. I'll make sure the dog is taken care of until she gets back, but be sure to tell her to call."

"She won't call," the woman assured me, puzzling over the paper the driver showed her. "She might come back, but she won't call."

I wanted to leave on a positive note, but I knew she was probably right.

"Well, if you want my opinion," announced my friend Maude a couple of days later, "that little collie has already found a good home."

I'd known Maude for most of my life, and she was, in many ways, as much of a mother to me as my own mother had been. When she spoke, I usually listened—in part because she had a clipped British accent that made every word she spoke sound more important than it was, and in part because she'd proven to be right about most things over the years. But not about this.

"I'm not looking for a dog," I told her firmly. "Besides, that collie is going to be easy to place. Look how nicely she cleaned up. Definitely a purebred. If I can get her picture in the paper this weekend, we'll have a dozen calls before Christmas."

Maude worked with me on the Humane Society, and I'd brought her out to the barn to have a look at the collie. I had fixed up one of the stalls in the barn for the dog, although, of course, I brought her in at night and let her sleep in a crate in the kitchen. Now she was contentedly curled up in a pile of hay, chewing a rubber bone.

The collie's owner had, in fact, actually called me... to surrender her dog. Though she'd been beside herself with amazed joy over the mysterious gift of a full propane tank, there had been tears in her voice, too, as she confessed she was no longer able to care for her dog. "I feel bad," she said, "but I know it's for the best. You try to give your children everything, but...when my four-year-old sat on Santa's lap all he wanted for Christmas was to go home and sleep in his own bed." She took a brave breath. "At least he's got that. I can only do the best I can."

A story like that made me ashamed of feeling sorry for myself, but I managed it anyway. "Besides," I said, turning to leave the barn, "I'm about to join the ranks of the unemployed. I can't take on another mouth to feed."

"Do you know, my dear," Maude said thoughtfully, glancing around the vast, dusty interior of the barn, "it would take almost nothing to convert this building into a functioning boarding kennel and training facility. Your father's horses always did live better than most families in this county... concrete floors, heating and plumbing already in place... the investment would be minimal for you. You already have more people asking you to teach classes than you can accommodate in the summer, and if you had an indoor facility, you could do it year around. You have room for twenty boarders, easily, and even at half capacity that would be a reasonable income."

I looked at her skeptically. "A boarding kennel is a lot of work."

"But there is something to be said for owning one's own business."

"I suppose." I couldn't believe I was actually considering it, however briefly. "And I do like teaching."

"You're quite good at it."

I returned a half-smile to the woman who'd been training me to train dogs since I was eight years old. "I learned from the best." And then I shrugged. "But there's no money in dog training. Besides…" My gaze slid away uncomfortably. "I don't have a dog."

Perhaps I should have mentioned that it had been Maude who'd given me my beloved Cassidy, a product of her own championship kennel, Sundance. I suspected in some ways losing Cassidy had been as hard on Maude as it had been on me, and I still couldn't mention Cassidy's name to Maude without tearing up.

Before that could happen, I added, "Anyway, I've got to get going. Aunt Mart talked me into being on the Families First Christmas Baskets committee, and we're meeting at the church to fill the baskets this afternoon. You'll put the word out about the collie, right?"

"I will. And you'll think about what I said?"

Because I wasn't entirely sure whether she was referring to what she'd said about the collie or about the kennel, I was careful to promise nothing except to call her later, and I hurried off to meet my aunt.

There was a Sheriff's Department patrol car in front of the church when I pulled in, and I naturally assumed it belonged to my uncle, who'd dropped Aunt Mart off for the meeting. I circled around to the basement door and parked beside the other vehicles, tucking my coat and scarf more securely around me as I got out into the cold. A moment later, I was stripping gloves, hat, scarf, and coat off as the blast of overheated air from inside the church basement hit me.

A dozen or so women were gathered in a long concrete-floored room to the left, and I could hear their voices as I approached.

"Absolutely scandalous, if you ask me. A man like that, running off with a woman half his age…"

For some reason, I always felt self-conscious when I heard the words "scandalous," "man," and "running off with a woman" in a sentence together… as though that sentence might in some way be referring to my failed marriage. So I entered the room hesitantly, stuffing my gloves into my coat pocket, only to be greeted by a cheerful, "Oh, hey Raine. We were just talking about that scamp Jess Hanson. Have you ever heard the like?"

Well, it's like my daddy always used to say: You wouldn't worry so much about what other people thought of you if you realized how seldom they did. My ex-husband Buck and I were old news by now. Of course I should have realized people had found something more interesting to talk about.

The room was lined with long tables, upon which were stacked piles of canned goods, packaged breads and cookies, canned hams, and straw baskets. The women had set up an assembly line, filling each basket with one item from the pile in front of them and topping it off with a red bow at the end. There were stacks of cardboard boxes from the food bank placed strategically around the room, and Aunt Mart was unpacking them.

"Well now, all I know is that Jess Hanson was a fine member of this community and an absolutely perfect Santa Claus for over sixty years," asserted Aunt Mart, pausing with her arms full of jellied cranberry sauce to offer her cheek for a kiss, which I obliged, "and if he wants to spend his sunset

Donna Ball

years in Jupiter Beach with that redhead, more
power to him. Hello, Raine, dear. At least we were
lucky enough to find someone to replace him."

I'd been a little self-involved the past few
months and wasn't entirely up on all the gossip,
but I gathered that Jess Hanson, who'd been the
town Santa for as long as I could remember, had
moved on to warmer pursuits. "So who's playing
Santa now?" I asked, hanging up my coat and
pushing up my sleeves. Since I was probably the
youngest person there, I figured my job would be
the heavy lifting, so I headed for the cardboard
boxes. "I was just by Hanson's Department Store
and there was some guy in a red suit sitting in the
window display with a line of children out the
door."

"Some fellow from up Raleigh way," answered
Donella Gray, mother of three. "He just moved
here last month. Retired carpenter, I think
somebody told me. To tell the truth, I like him a lot
better than Jess as Santa. That beard of his is real,
and the kids know the difference, let me tell you."

"He's been really nice about taking over all of
Jess's obligations, even the unpaid ones—the
school parties, the church pageant, and of course
he'll play Santa at the town Christmas party."

"I still think Jess Hanson had nerve."

The women worked and gossiped with equal energy, never missing a beat as they passed the baskets down the line to be filled. "Wow," I said, setting a heavy box of canned hams on the table. "This sure is a lot of stuff."

"Seventy-five baskets," replied Aunt Mart sadly, "and that doesn't even meet the need. It just breaks my heart, right here at Christmas time, to know all the families that are hurting. We're each going to take on delivering ten baskets. I was wondering, Raine, if you'd mind driving me in your car, since it's so much bigger?"

I said, "Sure, but isn't that why Uncle Roe's here? I saw his patrol car out front."

She looked surprised. "That's not Roe. He's got a lunch meeting with the mayor and you know those things always go on all afternoon." Then she glanced across the table and said, "Wait, Sara Lyn, first the creamed corn, then the green peas. You've got two cans of peas there."

Sara Lyn pointed out that she was out of creamed corn, and after a search through the boxes Aunt Mart sent me upstairs to make sure all the cartons had been brought down from the church office. That was when I met my ex-husband coming out of the administrative wing.

I should have mentioned that my ex is a deputy sheriff, and he'd worked for my uncle even longer than he'd been married to me. To say we now found ourselves in an awkward situation would be an understatement, and I wasn't just talking about meeting each other in the corridor of a church on a Wednesday afternoon.

Buck Lawson had the kind of lazy good looks that women found hard to resist—rumpled curly hair, kind hazel eyes, an easy smile, and a genuine interest in folks. Unfortunately, Buck found the admiration of women equally difficult to resist, which was where all his problems began, at least as far as I was concerned. We each came to a dead stop in the hallway about ten feet apart and stared at each other like a couple of deer in the headlights until I, determined to be the bigger person, cleared my throat a little and said, almost casually, "Hi, Buck. What are you doing here?"

He hesitated a moment, as though he wasn't quite sure of the answer to that, gave a little half-glance over his shoulder toward the office to orient himself, and answered, "Oh, we got a call. The love offering from the Christmas cantata was robbed, can you believe that? Four hundred and eighty-five dollars. The ░░░░░░░░ thing is, there was only five hundred and two dollars in the plate." He gave a small shake of his head. "I don't know what the world is coming to."

"Well, times are hard, I guess," I offered awkwardly.

"Syms Sporting Goods has been hit twice this month alone," he said. "It's got to where they don't even leave any cash in the register anymore. Of course, Lou Syms is such an old skinflint it's hard to feel sorry for him. But stealing from a church is something else."

We stood there for another uncomfortable moment, out of small talk, and then I blurted, "I just came up for corn."

And he said at the same time, "Raine, I need to talk to you about something."

We both broke off expectantly, and he looked embarrassed. "Look," he said, "your uncle invited me to Christmas dinner, just like always. I'm sure he wasn't thinking, but I told him no, of course. I just wanted you to know it wasn't because—well, because I was with someone else. I just didn't think it was right, that's all."

I swallowed hard. I had not yet been able to imagine what it would be like at the holiday table this year. None of my dad's corny jokes. No golden retriever hiding under the table waiting to filch pieces of turkey and homemade biscuits. No quiet shared smiles between me and the person who was supposed to have loved me for the rest of my life. I said, "Yeah. Okay."

"I volunteered to work on Christmas. You know, give the family guys a day off."

"That's good." My tone was stiff.

He looked bleak. "Raine, I don't think I can stand for you to hate me."

I thrust my hands into my pockets and managed to mutter, "I don't hate you." I wasn't entirely sure whether that was true.

He took a step toward me, his eyes softening in a way that made me wish I hadn't just told him I didn't hate him. "Raine, I am so sorry," he said. "I don't expect you to forgive me, but I just want you to know I understand what I've done to you, and if I could take it back I would. You deserve so much better. I'm just... so ▓▓▓▓ sorry."

The thing is, I knew he meant it. Every word. And listening to him just made me tired.

I said, "I'm glad you're sorry. I know you think that's supposed to make everything better. I trusted you, and you lied to me. You promised to be there for the rest of my life and now I'm all alone in that big house at Christmas. We said we'd take care of each other, and now I'm taking care of myself. But I'm glad you're sorry."

He dropped his gaze. "I don't suppose… do you ever see a time when we might be friends again?"

I said simply, "No." And I turned and walked back toward the basement. Let somebody else worry about the corn.

And that was when I heard a scream.

Buck had been a high school football hero — naturally — and he hadn't lost any speed over the years. He outran me to the vestibule, but not by much. That had been my aunt's voice I'd heard.

"Stop, thief! Stop!" she cried.

I arrived just as Buck was tackling a denim-jacketed man who was halfway out the door. "Tackle" might have been too strong a word. Buck's modus operandi has always been on the

Donna Ball

mild side, so it was more like he caught the guy casually by the elbow and the collar, turned him back into the room, and said, "Whoa, dude, what's your hurry?"

Meanwhile, I rushed to Aunt Mart, who'd grabbed an umbrella from the stand in the vestibule and held it like a baseball bat, her chest heaving with indignation and her eyes flashing at the perpetrator. My aunt was every bit the southern lady, but she'd been around law enforcement too long not to rise to the occasion when it counted.

"Aunt Mart, are you all right?" I put my hands around the umbrella and tried to gently take it from her, but she was having none of it.

"I'm fine," she returned shortly, tightening her grip on the umbrella. "But it's a good thing Buck got here when he did or that young man would not have been, I can assure you of that!" With a final warning look at the suspect in custody, she turned to me. "I came up to tell you we found the other cartons of corn, and I heard somebody creeping around up front, and I thought it might be one of the volunteers who was lost, so I peeked around the corner and what should I see but this—this *miscreant* trying to break into the tithe box!"

"I wasn't breaking in!" returned the miscreant in question angrily. The scattered bills all over the marble floor and the broken hinge on the tithe box would seem to belie his story, not to mention the wad of cash that was still clearly clutched in one hand.

Aunt Mart turned on him with eyes blazing and her chest heaving with righteous indignation, raising the umbrella another couple of threatening inches. "How dare you steal from the Lord in His own house! All that glitters is not gold, you know! Vengeance is mine, sayeth the Lord! And woe to that man who betrays the Son of Man! It would be better for him if he had not been born!"

By this time the pastor had arrived with his secretary, and between the three of us, we were able to persuade Aunt Mart to relinquish the umbrella. She did so with a dusting of her hands and a single tug at the hem of her jacket, and if Buck's grip had failed to hold the villain, her glare certainly would have.

He was a thin man in his late thirties with a prominent Adam's apple and lank brown hair falling over his eyes. He wore muddy work boots and faded jeans that were just this side of being threadbare. His jacket wasn't nearly warm enough to keep out the kind of cold we were expecting over the next few days. He was clearly such an amateur thief, and so clearly caught dead-to-rights, that I couldn't help feeling a little sorry for him.

"I wasn't breaking in," the man repeated, starting to sweat. "I know this looks bad, but I can explain."

"Maybe you can start by explaining this," Buck invited, nodding at the money on the floor. "And where did you get that cash in your hand there?"

"Well, it wasn't from the tithe box," said the secretary, looking both alarmed and slightly pleased with herself. "At least I don't see how it could be. I emptied it at one o'clock, just like I do every Wednesday, and unless we've had more drop-ins in the last half hour than we've had all week, this money didn't come from the box."

The pastor confirmed her claim, and the suspect practically sagged with relief. "I'm trying to tell you, I wasn't taking money out. I was trying..." His voice fell, and he looked embarrassed. I would have been embarrassed too, if I'd had such a lame story. "I was trying to put it back in."

My aunt and I exchanged a look. Even she, who always saw the best in everyone, wasn't buying this one. I felt so bad for the guy I couldn't even look at him, so I knelt down and started picking up the scattered bills. They were mostly ones, with a few fives here and there, exactly the kind of denominations you'd find in a donation box.

Buck said politely, "You want to explain all the money on the floor, Mr....?"

"It's Jacobs. Jim Jacobs," he said miserably. "Look, I don't expect you to believe me, but there's a hundred and ten dollars altogether, with what I dropped and what I still have." He opened his hand and Buck took the money he offered. I added my pile to it, and Buck passed the money to the pastor.

"I found it last night in my mailbox bound up in a rubber band with a note that said 'From your Secret Santa.'" Jacobs went on. "And when I heard on the radio this morning that the church had been robbed…"

Buck said, "You heard it on the radio?"

Now the pastor looked embarrassed. "Lenny Fox is the church treasurer," he explained. "Of course we called him first thing." Lenny Fox was also the morning announcer for our local AM station.

Jim Jacobs nodded, his Adam's apple bobbing. "The thing is, times have been a little rough for us since the plant closed, and we got the final notice on the electric bill, and my oldest boy, now I'm not saying he's no angel, but he's never been in any serious trouble with the law, but he must have heard us arguing about it, my wife and me—you know how folks do when times are bad—because he banged out of the house the other night saying something about how he was going to fix things, and the next I know there's this money in the mailbox, which is exactly what it would take to keep the lights on, so what am I supposed to think? He never would admit it, but I'm telling you , Deputy, we're an honest God-loving family and no son of mine is going to stand before his Maker with this on his conscience. So I came here to give the money back, only…" A dull flush crept up his collar. "The slot was too small and I was afraid if I stood here long enough to put it all in one bill at a time somebody would come by and see me and wonder where I got that kind of money to give to the church, so I tried to pull up the lid just enough to push the money through, but the hinge broke, and then…" His voice trailed off pitifully. We all knew what had happened next.

I felt compelled to speak up. "Listen, Buck, it probably doesn't mean anything, but he might be telling the truth about the Secret Santa thing." I told him about my experience with the propane truck driver, and a look of speculative interest lit the faces of everyone in the room—except Jim Jacobs, of course, who just looked miserable.

The pastor said, "Well, I for one am pleased to think there's a philanthropist in our midst, whether it's technically true or not." He offered the cash to Buck, neatly stacked and counted. "A hundred and ten dollars, just like he said. And I don't know of any law that prosecutes a man for trying to give money to the church."

Buck glanced down at the money. "I'm guessing you don't want to press charges for the broken box."

"You guess correctly."

Somewhat reluctantly, Buck released Jacobs's arm. "I'm going to want to talk to your son. Meantime…" He inclined his head toward the cash the pastor still held. "Looks to me like that belongs to the church."

That's the way things are handled in a small town.

My aunt thoughtfully surveyed the perpetrator, who hadn't yet completely grasped the fact that he was free. "Jacobs. Are you the James Jacobs with two children who lives out on Blackberry Mountain?"

He answered cautiously, "Yes, ma'am."

"Oh, for heaven's sake, you're on our list!" She turned to me and repeated, as though that explained everything, "He's on our list." She reached for his hand. "Come downstairs and have a hot cup of coffee and some cookies. We're going to fix up a box for you to take home to those children."

Like I said, that's the way things are done in a small town.

Over the next several days, stories began to pile up about the Secret Santa. At least a dozen of the recipients of our food baskets had also received a gift from Secret Santa—an envelope filled with cash for some; for one it had been a new water heater after being unable to replace the broken one for six months; one elderly woman who lived alone in a drafty old house had found a beautifully wrapped package containing an electric blanket on her porch—along with a note that read "from your Secret Santa." More than one family with small children had discovered that wrapped gifts with their children's names on them had been left by their door overnight, and the tag on each one read "from your Secret Santa." An excited buzz of speculation and anticipation started to build throughout the town as everyone tried to guess the philanthropist's identity… and secretly hoped they might be the next object of his generosity.

"It's like that billionaire in Kansas City who went around giving hundred-dollar bills to the homeless."

"Or that fellow in L.A. who dropped cash from a helicopter."

"Or that guy that travels to a different city every Christmas, handing out cash in the projects."

My aunt didn't think it was any of those. "One person couldn't do all of this," she maintained. "It simply has to be a group, like the Boy Scouts or the Knights of Columbus."

I said, "I wonder how he knows what everyone needs."

"I shouldn't imagine it would be that difficult," observed Maude. "All one would need is a glimpse at the case file from one of any number of charitable organizations."

Maude, Aunt Mart, and I were on our way home from the Women's Club Christmas Gala, at which a lot of cheese puffs had been eaten and a lot of fruit punch consumed, an endless list of thank yous had been read, and a program involving the middle school chorale had been presented. I'm not a member of the Women's Club and their meetings are usually the kind of thing I'd fake a case of the flu to avoid attending, but my aunt had invited me as part of her keep-Raine-busy campaign, and I just didn't have the energy to refuse. Maude, who was a member of the Women's Club but rarely actually attended meetings, had come along for moral support.

Naturally, Secret Santa had been a subject of gossip and speculation at the meeting. Everyone had a story; no one had a clue. My favorite theory, however, was the one involving the head of the textile plant who had suddenly found Jesus/a conscience/a desperate need to redeem himself after putting so many people out of work and plunging the county into a premature economic depression.

I said with a sigh, "Well, whoever he is, I sure wish he'd pay me a visit."

My aunt, who was driving, laughed lightly. "Honey, don't we all? Why, only the other day…" Suddenly she hit the brakes so hard that my seat belt locked. "Good heavens, are those foxes?"

"No," said Maude, twisting in her seat to look out the window. "They're puppies."

But I'd already unfastened my seat belt and was scrambling out the back door, hurrying toward the two small gray forms gamboling along the side of the road and into the path of traffic. I scooped up the pups before they could make a fatal mistake, and I recall the amusement in Maude's tone as she observed, "Maybe he already has."

A couple of hours later, two gorgeous blue merle Australian shepherd puppies were making themselves at home in the hay-lined stall next to the young collie. They were mirror opposites of each other—one with a patch over the left eye, the other with a patch over the right—both perfect little females about twelve weeks old. "I can't believe people sometimes," I said, fuming. "Just look at those pups. Natural bobbed tails, perfect fold on the ears... Who would just toss them out? I mean, look at them!"

"Gorgeous," agreed Maude. "But times are difficult for everyone. Perhaps whoever abandoned them was hoping they were setting them free to find the perfect home." She looked at me meaningfully.

"Oh, for heaven's sake." I gave an impatient shake of my head. "I told you, I'm not ready for a dog."

"When will you be ready?" asked Maude reasonably.

I frowned uncomfortably. "I don't know. Maybe never."

"I don't believe that for a moment." Maude's gaze was steady and compassionate. "Raine," she said, "you're punishing yourself for something that wasn't your fault. Cassidy lived a full, long life, and it was her time to go. Someone else chose to end your marriage. You didn't. Your father wouldn't have wanted you to keep this place like a museum to honor him. He would want you to live in every inch of it. You need to get on with it."

She was really starting to annoy me on the subject. "Look, I can barely take care of myself, much less a dog," I told her. "If I read my own application on a pet adoption form, I'd turn it down. Besides, you know what they say… when the time is right, the right dog will appear."

"A collie and two Australian shepherds have already appeared," she pointed out. "What more do you want?"

I blinked back a surprising hotness in my eyes, and the anger in my voice was both unexpected and embarrassing. "I want Cassidy back," I said tightly. "I want to have Christmas dinner with my dad one more time. I want my husband to keep his marriage vows. And right now, I want to find a home for these puppies." I turned on my heel and walked away.

I advertised the dogs on the radio and in the paper. I had several calls about the Aussie puppies, but most people wanted only one and the pups were so obviously attached to each other—not only littermates, but twins—that I hated to break up the pair unless I absolutely had to. A couple of people were interested in the collie, but when I interviewed them, I knew she would just be going to sit atop another dog house in another muddy ten-by-ten pen. Perhaps the hardest thing I had to do was turn people down because they couldn't afford the adoption fee, which was just enough to cover the cost of shots and spay/neuter surgery, which our vet performed at his own cost. In the case of the puppies, that came to sixty-six dollars and fifty cents each; for the collie, it was slightly less. On more than one occasion, I was tempted to waive the fee, but the humane society had a strict policy and I had to honor it—particularly since I was the one who'd written the policy. Besides, I was as unemployed as everyone else in the county, and I couldn't afford to pay the fee out of my own pocket.

And then I had an excited call from a young mother who wanted to get one of the puppies for her ten-year-old son, but who, upon learning of the fee, had hung up in disappointment before I could even add that I was looking to place the puppies together. "It's a miracle," she exclaimed, barely pausing to remind me who she was, "an absolute Christmas miracle! I mean, I heard about that woman that got her rent paid just when she was about to be kicked out on the street, and you heard about Craig Killian's transmission going out and

him with no way to get to work over in Wilford
and then the very next day he got four hundred
eighty-five dollars in the mail—which is just what
it was going to cost to fix his car! I know it's
happening all over town, but I never expected it to
happen to me—to us—to Nick. All he's been asking
for all year was a puppy for Christmas, and when I
told him we couldn't afford the fee he was so
disappointed that I just didn't know what we were
going to do. Johnson tried to get extra shifts down
at the gas station, and I started asking around to
see if somebody didn't need their house cleaned for
Christmas, but you know how it is this time of
year. Nobody has any extra cash… until I looked in
the mailbox this morning and what did I see but an
envelope from Secret Santa with—this is the
miracle part!—exactly sixty-six dollars and fifty
cents in it!"

"Wow," I said, impressed. "That is a miracle."

"And even though Johnson says we could buy
Nicky a lot of Christmas toys for that much money,
what he wants is a puppy, so I knew I had to call
you back. The only thing is, we were hoping to get
something with a little less hair, and Nick has
always wanted a dog like Snoopy. I don't guess
you'd have any beagles, would you?"

I told her I wasn't sure, but gave her the telephone number of our foster home coordinator, secretly a little glad she hadn't taken one of the Aussies, after all. Like I said, I hated to break them up.

I was still puzzling over the whole thing—sixty-six dollars and fifty cents *exactly*—as I drove into town to meet my uncle for our annual lunch and shopping trip to pick out Aunt Mart's Christmas present. And it wasn't just the adoption fee. What was it about the story about Craig Killian's transmission that was bothering me?

By the time I reached my uncle's office in the Public Safety Building, I thought I had it figured out.

There was a fruit-studded wreath on the front door and garlands over the doorways, courtesy of the Hanover County Beautification Society, but otherwise it was pretty much business as usual at the Sheriff's Department. I greeted the girl at the front desk and said hello to Wyn, Buck's partner, who was typing up a report. They told me I could find my uncle in the meeting room. I started back and then hesitated. "Is Buck around?"

"He's taking some personal time," answered the receptionist and then held up a finger as she took a call. "Sheriff's Department."

"He said he was working on a Christmas present for someone special," volunteered Wyn from her computer station and then immediately looked embarrassed. We both knew, this year, that someone special would not be me.

I spoke quickly over my own discomfort, trying to sound casual. "Say, Wyn, did you work the church case with Buck? You know, the cantata robbery?"

She shook her head and swiveled her chair toward me, eager to make amends. "I was on desk duty that day, trying to catch up on the paperwork. I swear, I've never seen such a Christmas for robberies and petty theft. Why? Something I can help you with?"

"I was just trying to remember how much was taken, exactly."

She turned to her computer and typed a few keys. "Four hundred eighty-five dollars," she said. "Apparently the offering plate was left unattended in the church office for about ten minutes while the usher took pictures for the church bulletin." She scrolled down a screen. "The thief didn't get it all, though. He must have heard someone coming and skedaddled."

"Any suspects?"

"Nah. There were almost three hundred people there that night. They had Santa Claus for the kids and a big buffet supper afterwards… I hate this kind of case. It could have been anybody." She looked up from the screen. "How come?"

"Nothing really, just an idea I had. Thanks, Wyn." Thoughtfully, I went in search of my uncle.

I found him in the meeting room, as directed, standing in front of a white board with his hands clasped behind his back. The board was filled with sloppy squares, pointy stars, and looped arrows, which I gradually began to understand was a diagram of some sort, and my uncle was gazing at it with studied absorption.

I said, "Hi, Uncle Roe. About ready for lunch?"

He gave a small shake of his head. "I just can't see it. There's got to be a pattern, but I can't figure it out."

I moved closer to the board as he pointed. "The Salvation Army kettle outside Hanson's department store—hit twice. Three ladies had their wallets emptied—not credit cards, just cash—from the Cash-n-Carry. Cash registers hit all over town, not just once, but randomly over the past month. And these guys are smart, too—they don't take everything at once, but leave a little behind so the robbery isn't noticed right away. All the churches have been hit. And the hospital fund and the Red Cross collection boxes. And"—his voice rose in indignation—"just last night The Empty Stocking Fund, if you can believe that. They got sixty-six dollars—"

"And fifty cents," I said softly, and he turned to look at me sharply. "Uncle Roe, I think I know who the thief is."

"So Secret Santa is actually Robin Hood," said Maude with a small shake of her head. "Whoever would have guessed?"

"Robin Hood, my eye," replied Sarabeth Potts with a sniff. "Robin Hood took from the rich to give to the poor. I don't know what you call somebody who takes from churches and Salvation Army kettles."

"Do you mean besides a thief?" said someone else, and we all laughed a little, though without much humor.

There were five of us setting up the Humane Society's adoption corner for the town Christmas party, which was really just an excuse to get shoppers downtown on this last weekend before Christmas in hopes that a little more cash would find its way into the hands of local businessmen. All the shops were gaily decorated and offering cookies and hot cider all day long, along with today-only discounts and door prizes. There were carolers and raffles and special performances by the various choirs , as well as scheduled appearances by Santa Claus around town. Uncle Roe had a full contingent of deputies working security for the event, and though he was usually a stickler for maintaining the dignity of law enforcement, on this occasion he'd bowed to the pressure of the Downtown Business Association and issued red Santa Claus hats to all his officers.

The Humane Society was always given a prime spot on the town square next to the Christmas tree, and this year we'd also been able to book a photographer for a "have your pet's picture taken with Santa" session. In the spirit of the event, all the volunteers wore jaunty elf hats and "Spay or Neuter Your Pet" buttons in Christmas colors. We were the last stop for Santa photos before the big day, and we'd already sold thirty tickets at $5.00 a pop.

"Anyway," I added, "keep your eye on the collection jar. Knowing *what* he is isn't the same as knowing *who* he is. The sheriff's department has been trying to interview everyone who got a gift from Secret Santa, but so far no suspects."

"Does that surprise you?" said Callie Anders, the photographer, who was busy setting up her faux-painted foam-core Christmas backdrop while the rest of us lugged heavy wire cages and ex-pens across the street to the town square. When I looked at her with what may have been a skeptically raised eyebrow, she explained, "I mean, really, the sheriff's department expects these people to give up the person who saved their Christmas? Even if they did know who it was, they wouldn't tell."

To tell the truth, I hadn't thought about that. Now I did.

"Merry Christmas, ladies!" A strong gloved hand fell on my shoulder and on the shoulder of the woman working next to me. I twisted around to look into the twinkling blue eyes of Santa Claus. He had a strong booming voice and an electric presence that, I had to admit, took me aback for a moment. "You know Santa has a special place in his heart for those who take care of his smallest elves, don't you?"

Okay, that made me smile. I transferred the two wriggling Australian shepherds into their temporary straw-lined pen and replied, "I hope that means Santa has already found a home for these puppies."

When I straightened up from placing the pups in the pen, he was smiling at me kindly. "Don't worry," he said. "When the time is right, the right dog will appear."

I felt a tingly sensation all over, and for a moment I couldn't think of what to say. Callie came up and touched his shoulder, pointing out the sheet-draped chair where he would be posing for photos with the pets, and I grabbed Maude's arm. "Did you tell him to say that?" I demanded, half whispering.

She had a black mutt on a leash in one hand and a pointer/hound mix tugging at the leash on the other, and she looked mildly baffled. "Tell who to say what?"

I whirled around to point at Santa, but he'd moved off into the crowd. I muttered something unintelligible and hurried off with my head down to help unload the rest of the animals for adoption into the display.

We adopted six animals—four kittens and two puppies—to new homes and had a steady stream of pets and pet owners lined up to have their pictures taken with Santa Claus. The mother and son who'd called me about their Christmas miracle came by to have their beagle-mix puppy's picture taken with Santa and left an extra $2.00 in the donation box. The beagle would probably grow up to be a coon hound, but the young boy loved it, and in this business that's all that matters. We collected over two hundred dollars from the photos, and everyone who stopped by would stuff another dollar or two into our plastic dog-shaped collection jar. As busy as I was, I made sure that jar was never out of my sight, or the sight of one of the volunteers, and at the end of the day I counted three hundred twenty-six dollars in bills and another twenty or so in change. I left the change in the jar and slipped a rubber band around the bills, handing it all over to Sarabeth Potts, our treasurer.

"If you leave now you can get this to the bank before it closes," I told her. "We've only got a few more pictures with Santa and then we're going to start packing up."

She tucked the envelope into her purse and zipped it up securely. "Okay, give me five minutes to give Santa a hand with that little dachshund. He already tried to bite one of the girls."

I grimaced. "Santa or the dog?"

"Very funny."

"Do you need any help?"

"No, I've got it," she called back over the sound of excited high-pitched barking and moved to Santa's station to calm the sharp-toothed dachshund.

The picture was taken without incident, and Sarabeth reported that Santa had been a good sport about the whole thing as she hurried off to the bank. The rest of us congratulated ourselves on a successful day as we started to pack up. The crowds had begun to thin, the apple cider and hot chocolate was running low, and the setting sun painted the sky overhead a dusky orange. The temperature had started to drop and, despite their warm beds filled with shredded newspaper and the furniture pads that shielded the crates from the wind, I didn't want to keep the animals out in the cold much longer. There were only a couple of people left in line for Santa photos, and while Cassie set up her last shots, I started to break down the adoption station.

"I can't believe no one was interested in those cute puppies," I said, looking in dismay at my two Aussies. We'd decided against bringing the collie to Adoption Day, since there was a good chance the children of the original owner might spot her, but I'd really thought the Australian shepherd pups would find a home today.

"It's not that no one was interested," Maude pointed out, "but that no one qualified. At least according to your standards."

I drew a breath to challenge her on that, but a voice from behind me stopped my thought.

"Raine? Got a minute?"

I turned to see Buck coming toward me. He was wearing a fleece-lined denim jacket over his uniform and had a red Santa's hat sticking out his back pocket. In his arms he carried a medium-sized cardboard box, and on his face was an expression that was about as uncomfortable as I'd ever seen. He glanced beyond me at Maude and then back to me.

Donna Ball

"When Roe said I could find you here, I didn't know…" His gazed swept the surroundings, puppy cages, Santa, and all, and grew even more uncomfortable. "This probably isn't the best time, but I go on duty in ten minutes and, well, I brought you something."

He set the box on the ground, but before he could lift the lid, it toppled to the ground of its own accord. Two fuzzy golden paws and a tiny golden retriever face with charcoal nose and chocolate eyes appeared over the edge of the box. I heard Maude gasp softly behind me, and when I glanced at her I saw that her lips were pressed tightly together and sealed by two fingers; Otherwise, she was expressionless. I may have mentioned that Maude is British and doesn't express emotions easily. But in this case, she didn't have to. I looked at the puppy and I knew exactly what she was thinking. I hadn't seen anything so beautiful since the day I had first looked at Cassidy.

The puppy tumbled out of the box with its jingle bell collar jingling and its red leash trailing behind it. I sank to my knees and caught the leash before the pup could scamper away into the crowd, "Oh," I gasped. "Oh, Maude, will you look at this? Look at his head, his eyes, those perfect little ears—

322

this pup is conformation ready! Who breeds goldens like this around here? Buck, where did you get him? Oh, never mind, I don't want to know. I'd just have to go to jail for beating up the person who abandoned this precious puppy and that would ruin everybody's Christmas..." By then I was snuggling the pup next to my face and his sharp little teeth were alternating between chewing on my chin and chewing on his leash. "But we're getting ready to close down here," I said, glancing around anxiously. "Why didn't you bring him in earlier?"

I heard Maude say softly, "Oh my word. You did it. You found him."

The pup had clamped on to the pompom of my elf hat and dragged it off my head. Laughing, I let him have the hat and watched as he attacked it with a little puppy growl and shook it with all the ferocity of a T-Rex taking out a saber-toothed tiger. I stood up, holding on to the leash, and Buck's expression, as he watched the puppy's antics, was even odder than it had been before—something of a mix between amusement, indulgence, embarrassment, and uncertainty.

He said, "Raine, I didn't exactly bring the pup for the adoption day. What I mean to say is…" He fumbled in his pocket and brought out an envelope, which he handed to me. "He has papers. And a registered name, if you're interested. It's Cassidy's Sundance Rides Again."

I just stared at him, not reacting at all, but I remember thinking from out of nowhere, *The Cisco Kid.* I looked down at the pup, who was now on his belly, shredding my hat into a pile of yarn and fuzz between his paws, and I knew that was his name. Cisco.

Maude came up beside me quietly. "Buck asked for a list of the owners of all Cassidy's pups," she said. "I didn't know why."

"I found one of them in Ohio," he said, "and they had one pup left from their last litter. It seemed like it was meant to be."

Okay, there was so much I could have said. In the first place, you never, ever give a puppy as a present—particularly to someone who doesn't know the puppy is coming and who hasn't asked for it. Seriously. Buck knew better. In the second place, here we were in the middle of a Humane Society Adoption Day with at least a half dozen puppies we couldn't find homes for, and he'd brought me yet another puppy all the way from Ohio. Really?

And in the third place... Cassidy's grandpup. He'd gone all the way to Ohio to find Cassidy's grandpup. The Cisco Kid.

The Cisco Kid had made mincemeat of my hat and now started in on my shoelaces. Before I could do so, Maude bent down and scooped him up. "Come along, young master," she said, "let's go have our photo taken, shall we?"

And then there was just Buck and me, standing a few awkward feet apart, looking at each other. I clutched the envelope with Cisco's papers in my hands. I wanted to be mad. I wanted to be defensive. I couldn't think of a single thing to say.

So Buck spoke first. "Look, I thought about what you said. None of this is your fault. I'm the one who screwed up. You didn't do anything wrong, and you ended up alone, and it's not right. So..." He shifted his gaze briefly, searching for words. "I know it's not enough, but... maybe it's a start. Somebody to watch over you, you know, and maybe do a better job than I did."

My heart gave a little twist in my chest. Out of the corner of my eye, I saw Santa trying to maintain his cheery composure while Cisco chewed on his beard, clawed at his buttons, and burrowed into his pockets. Callie laughed out loud as she snapped photos, and Maude tried her best to try to keep the puppy still for the camera.

I said, "Buck..." And I had no idea what would follow that.

That was probably a good thing, because at that moment chaos broke loose. There was a cry and a crash, and I spun around to see that the golden puppy had somehow managed to catch in his teeth the white sheet that had covered Santa's throne and tug the chair over, bringing with it a table, a small decorated tree, and a basket of dog treats. Santa, Maude, and the photographer were scrambling to untangle the pup from the fabric, while the puppies in the nearby ex-pens jumped and barked and clawed at their wire confines, trying to get to the spilled treats that Cisco was gobbling as fast as he could find them. Passing dogs sensed the excitement and pulled their owners toward the fray. I turned to help, and so did Buck, but just then someone grabbed my shoulder from behind.

"Oh, Raine!" Sarabeth looked distraught. "Raine, I don't know what to do. I've looked everywhere! I don't know how it happened. I had my purse with me the whole time..." Suddenly she noticed Buck and the uniform under his jacket. "Oh, officer, thank goodness! The money is gone! I got to the car and opened my purse for my keys and the envelope wasn't there! I think…" She looked horrified as the truth settled over her. "I think someone picked my pocket!"

Buck said, in that calm, authoritative way he has, "Tell me exactly what happened."

I opened my mouth to help out, but just then Maude called, "Raine, can you give us a hand here?"

I looked from the crisis in front of me to the crisis to the left of me, decided that Buck could handle this one for a few minutes by himself, and ran to help untangle Santa from a red leash, a mountain of cotton batting that had been shredded to look like snow, and a very slippery golden retriever puppy.

"We are so sorry!" I gasped, finally reeling in the little pup from underneath the chair, where he'd located one last dog biscuit. "Wouldn't you know? On your last picture of the day. You've been so nice to do this for us. I can't tell you how much we appreciate it."

But Santa was laughing good-naturedly. "Not a problem, young lady. My pleasure. Who could ask for a better job than this? Sitting around all day making children's dreams come true? Of course, in the case of this young fellow…" His eyes actually twinkled as he looked at the puppy, who'd settled into my arms and started chewing on one of my curls. "I'd say his dreams have already come true." He clucked the puppy under the chin with his index finger and winked at me. "You know what they say—all that glitters is usually golden."

I quickly set the puppy on the ground, holding on tightly to the leash, and Santa shook hands all around while we gushed our gratitude again. He bent to pet Cisco, and the puppy bounded up and bumped Santa on the nose, hard enough to hurt. But Santa just laughed it off, moving away through the crowd, waving and ho-ho-hoing.

"We should have paid him something," Cassie said. "That's the best Santa we ever had."

"We can't, even if we wanted to." I saw no reason to postpone the inevitable, and my tone was glum. "The money's gone."

I tried to explain amidst their gasps and questions, but it wasn't easy to do with the puppy bouncing and tugging at the end of the leash and winding himself beneath my feet. Sarabeth was still talking to Buck and looking as though she was about to cry, and I knew we should go over and comfort her. I bent down to scoop up the puppy, who'd found something on the ground and was methodically shredding it with his teeth. It was at that moment I realized I no longer held the envelope with the puppy's registration papers in my hand. "Oh, no!" I cried and bent to snatch the half-shredded envelope from the puppy's mouth.

"Oh dear," said Maude. "I thought I saw him pull something out of Santa's pocket. Is it ruined?"

I glanced at her in confusion, for in the dim light it was difficult to be certain what I'd rescued from the puppy until I actually held it in my hand, and even then I stared at it for another moment before I was certain. The envelope didn't contain AKC papers. "Sarabeth!" I cried excitedly. "Buck! It's here! It's okay. I found it!"

I finished what the puppy's sharp teeth had started, tearing open the envelope to reveal the cash inside. A few bills fluttered to the ground when I did so, and Maude dived to pick them up before the puppy could. Sarabeth cried out loud in relief when she saw the cash. "Oh, thank goodness! It's a miracle! I don't know what I would have done if I'd really lost that money. Where did you find it?"

"Make sure it's all there," Buck suggested. "Where'd you find it, Raine?"

"She didn't find it," Callie explained, laughing. "The puppy did. As a matter of fact…"

I looked up from counting the money. "It's all here," I said, puzzled, turning the money over to Sarabeth. "Plus sixty-two more."

"Eighty-three," said Maude, handing her a twenty and a one that she'd pried out of the puppy's mouth.

Sarabeth stared at the bills. "Wait a minute," she said. "There are six twenties here. We collected mostly fives and a few ones." She looked up, confusion and distress marring her relief. "I don't think this is our money."

Maude's expression was grim. "Plus this."

She had a folded piece of paper in her hand, and she gave it to Buck. He looked at it, then at her. "Where did you find this?"

She nodded to the puppy, who was busily sniffing the ground for something else to chew. "I think it fell out of the envelope with some of the bills. The pup was about to chew it."

I craned my neck to look at the paper. "From your Secret Santa," I read out loud.

It took a moment for us to get it. I stared at Sarabeth. "You were helping Santa with the dachshund right after I gave you the envelope."

I turned quickly to Maude. "And you said the puppy pulled this envelope out of Santa's pocket?"

Buck said, "Sounds to me like I need to have a chat with Mr. Claus."

I scanned the crowd until I spotted a familiar red hat. "There he is!"

Buck moved quickly in the direction I pointed, and I scooped up the puppy and hurried to keep up. This was one interview I had no intention of missing.

"Think about it," I said as we wound through the revelers toward the red hat. "He was always in the right place at the right time. Hanson's Department Store, Syms Sporting Goods, the Christmas Cantata. Every fund-raising event and public party in the county! And who would suspect Santa Claus?"

Buck glanced at me, and I could tell his mind was working along the same track. "He always left a little something behind," he muttered.

"Only when he didn't need it all," I pointed out. My excitement and my outrage grew as I added, "And how did he know what people needed? The kids told him! He just two minutes ago said he spent all day making dreams come true. All he'd have to do is ask the right questions."

"Hey!" Buck shouted, pressing forward, and a tall man in a red Santa hat turned. It was only Mike, one of Buck's fellow deputies. Buck swore under his breath.

"What's up?" Mike asked.

"We're looking for Santa Claus," I answered, gasping a little as we reached him.

Mike chuckled. "Who isn't? Cute dog," he added.

"Thanks," I said, and the puppy, who was grinning happily with the excitement of the chase, licked my face. "Big man, red suit."

"No kidding, man," Buck said. "Have you seen him?"

"Yeah, he was here a minute ago." Mike looked around. "There he is, headed toward Hanson's." He pointed across the street.

The Christmas lights started to come on all over town as we dashed across Main Street: the wreaths and candy canes that decorated the lamp posts, the swags that were draped over the shop doors, the miniature trees in the store windows. The Christmas village in front of the florist's shop sprang to multicolored life as we ran past, and I slowed my step a little for one more appreciative look. The big tree in the town square lit up in a cascade of red and blue and green, and a dozen sparkling red and white wreaths blinked on along the front of Hanson's Department store. On the roof of the store, the north pole came to life with snow men, elves, reindeer, and dancing nutcrackers. The whole world was bathed in color, and somewhere a choir was singing, "Hark, the Herald Angels." The puppy twisted this way and that in my arms, his excited panting hot against my cheek, trying to take in everything.

"There he is!" I cried, and this time it was really him, just reaching the corner of the block that ended in a blind alley behind Hanson's.

"Hey!" Buck called. "Hey, wait up a minute!"

Santa turned, saw us, and lifted his hand in a wave. "Merry Christmas!" he called back.

"Hold on! We need to talk to you!"

But Santa didn't stop. In fact, he might have increased his pace a little as he turned the corner into the alley. And what was Buck supposed to do? Pull a gun on Santa Claus? With frustration tight on his face, he ran after him.

Santa couldn't have been more than fifteen or twenty steps ahead of him, and as I've said, Buck was fast. I wasn't so fast, particularly when weighed down by a bouncy puppy, and I burst into the alleyway, gasping for breath, a second or two behind Buck.

The alley was—except for Buck, the puppy, and me—empty.

Long ago, perhaps in the days of wagons, the fifteen by fifteen area had been used as a loading dock. Now it was nothing but a concrete walled space with no practical purpose that contained nothing but a few rotting wood pallets and a crushed gallon paint bucket. The reflected Christmas lights from the roof illuminated the small area as brightly as daytime. Nonetheless, Buck took out his flashlight and shone it on every square and empty inch.

I lowered the puppy to the ground, easing my aching arms, bending at the waist to catch my breath. "He was… right here," I insisted, wheezing a little. "I saw him!"

Buck frowned. "Me, too." His flashlight beam climbed the solid wall, at least a story and a half high. "Damned if I know how he got out of here."

"Reindeer?"

Buck turned to me, about to make some equally sarcastic remark, and then stopped, listening. I heard it, too. For a moment we just stared at each other, and then, slowly, raised our eyes to the sky, looking for the source of the sound that simply couldn't be mistaken for anything else. It was the crisp, clear sound of jingling sleigh bells.

That was the last we ever heard of Santa Claus.

"**A**w, come on," said Melanie. Her eyes were big behind her black-rimmed glasses and tinged with healthy skepticism. "You don't really expect me to believe that."

"It's true," said Buck, who shared a wink with me over Melanie's head. "I was there."

The room had begun to fill up while I talked, although we were still a few minutes away from the official opening of the doors. Maude had brought young Pepper in from the grooming room, freshly styled and shining like silk, with a red and white bow clipped behind each ear and nails that were painted, at Melanie's insistence, bright red. My Aunt Mart arrived in a festive "Deck the Halls with Bows of Collies" Christmas sweater and Majesty the collie on a leash. Majesty looked equally festive in a gold-trimmed red velvet ruffled collar and was still every bit as imperious as she'd been the day I'd first met her, sitting atop a dog house in a muddy lot. Buck had stopped by with a fifty-pound sack of dog food that the boys from the department had donated for the animal shelter and had stayed to repair a malfunctioning strand of lights and to tack up the sagging garland over the doorway. My twin blue merle Aussies, Mischief and Magic, had come in from the play yard calm enough to allow Melanie to wrestle them into Santa Claus hats and now wandered happily around the room, each with a hat under her chin, looking for trouble to get into.

Cisco had, of course, bounded from his mat the moment Buck opened the door, slinging himself into his hero's arms. Buck and I had been more or less amicably divorced for years now, but Buck was still Cisco's favorite person in the world. I sometimes thought he knew, somewhere deep in his doggie heart, that Buck was the one who'd brought us together and changed both our lives. Now he pranced around the room like the gracious host and more or less model citizen he was, plumed tail waving, reminding everyone with his ineffable grin that it was, indeed, the season to be jolly.

"Seriously," Melanie said, "you caught him, right?"

"Wish I could say so," Buck admitted. "The sheriff's department over in Broward did pick up a fellow with the same MO a few weeks later, but something happened with the evidence and they had to let him go."

"And no one was ever able to tie those crimes with the ones here," said Maude. "If indeed you could call them crimes."

"Of course they were crimes," I said indignantly. "He stole three hundred twenty-six dollars from us!"

"But we received four hundred nine in return," Maude pointed out. "No one ever claimed the envelope Cisco found, so all the money went to the Humane Society."

"The worst part probably was that I never found Cisco's registration papers," I told Melanie. "My guess is I dropped them in all the confusion, and the phony Santa picked up the envelope thinking it was the one that had the money in it. I wish I could've seen his face when he opened up the envelope."

"All you have to do is write to the AKC for a copy," said Melanie who, thanks to the Internet, knew a little bit about everything.

"Which I did," I assured her.

"I never heard any more about the man, did you?" Aunt Mart came in with a bowl of ice cubes for the punch. "The most peculiar case I think Roe ever had."

"There was no sleigh in that alley," Melanie insisted determinedly. She straightened one of the bows behind Pepper's ear, which had already been dislodged a half dozen times in puppy play.

"Then how did he get out?" Buck queried, straight-faced.

"And what about the sleigh bells?" I added.

"Aren't you planning to be a detective when you grow up?" asked Maude.

"FBI," I corrected.

"Well then," said Buck, "this sounds to me like the kind of case a future FBI agent in training should be able to figure out."

Melanie said thoughtfully, "Yeah." Then, more confidently, "Yeah, I will. Don't you worry about that." She turned to walk away, then looked back at me. "You know," she said, "I'm glad the Forest Service downsized you. If they hadn't, you never would have opened Dog Daze. And if you hadn't opened Dog Daze, you never would have met my dad, and…" She shrugged. "Funny how things work out, huh?"

I didn't bother to point out that the way I had met her dad had been far, far more complicated than she made it sound. That was a story for another day. I agreed simply, "Right. Funny."

"But there was no sleigh in that alley," she repeated sternly. She walked away, pondering, while the rest of us shared a grin.

Aunt Mart slipped her arm through Buck's. "Buck, honey, I know you've got to get back to work but if I could steal you and that hammer of yours for just one more minute, I really don't like the way that tree is tilting to the left…"

She led him off, and I wandered, drawn by the pull of exquisite party food aromas, toward my office for a quick taste of what was cooking before everyone else arrived. The best thing about Melanie's dad, Miles—aside from the fact that he was inexplicably wild about me—was that he was a great cook and he didn't mind who knew it. Thanks to him, this year the Dog Daze Christmas party would include garlic shrimp, non-alcoholic eggnog, and some kind of incredible melty cheese wrapped in bacon on toast points for the adults, along with the cookies and punch for the children.

I opened the door to my bright blue and yellow office, where the food prep stations had been staged, and he turned, a spatula in one hand, wearing a Santa hat and an apron decorated with dancing elves. He deadpanned, "Do you think this outfit is emasculating?"

The other great thing about Miles is that he makes me laugh way, way more than he makes me cry, which, all things considered, makes my relationship with him the best one I've ever had with anyone except Cisco. I went into his arms and kissed his lips, which tasted of garlic shrimp and white wine sauce. He leaned his forehead against mine, looked deep into my eyes, and said softly, "There was no sleigh in that alley."

Someone put on the Bow-Wow Baritone's version of "Jingle Bells" (easily recognizable, since the lyrics are "woof-woof- woof"), and Miles and I carried out platters of hors d'oeuvres to the buffet table. The jingle bells over the door rang repeatedly as one dog after another tugged his owner excitedly inside—terriers, hounds, toys and mutts, all dressed in their Christmas finery, accompanied by men, women and children of all ages. Someone gave Cisco a dog-bone shaped present wrapped in gold, with which he pranced around proudly, teasing the other dogs, until Pepper grabbed one end of it and a tug of war ensued. The stuffed toy inside was ignored for the gold ribbon that came on the package, and Maude snapped pictures of the two golden retrievers playing tug of war with the ribbon.

"All that glitters is usually golden," I said, grinning as I watched them.

The jingle bells sounded again and a yellow lab bounded in. Melanie, who was untangling Pepper's paws from the ribbon, looked up at the bells, then at me. She burst into laughter. "I've got it!" she cried. "It was Cisco's jingle bell collar that you heard! He was wearing a jingle bell collar in the picture, and when you put him down he probably started scratching. It wasn't sleigh bells at all—it was Cisco!"

Miles brought me a glass of eggnog, and I lifted it to Melanie in a salute. "Good for you. You'll be taking your Detective First Class exam before you know it."

She nodded smugly. "I told you there was no sleigh in that alley." She picked up the stuffed toy Cisco had dropped and started to toss it to him, then hesitated, frowning at me a little. "Then how did Santa get out of the alley?"

I just smiled.

Melanie tossed the toy for Cisco, still looking thoughtful. Cisco leapt to catch it and took off at a dash, leading the charge toward the playroom. Dogs barked, children laughed, music played, lights twinkled. A mastiff stepped on my foot, and an Australian shepherd leapt onto the table and dunked a paw into the punch bowl. The Christmas tree swayed dangerously.

And in the background, the sound of sleigh bells still could be heard.

High in Trial

Also in The Raine Stockton Dog Mystery Series

Spine-chilling suspense by Donna Ball

Donna Ball

built their luxury homes in the heart of virgin forest they did not realize that something was there before them... something ancient and horrible; something that will make them believe that monsters are real.

EXPOSURE
Everyone has secrets, but when talk show host Jessamine's Cray's stalker begins to use her past to terrorize her, no one is safe ... not her family, her friends, her coworkers, and especially not Jess herself.

RENEGADE by Donna Boyd
Enter a world of dark mystery and intense passion, where human destiny is controlled by a species of powerful, exotic creatures. Once they ruled the Tundra, now they rule Wall Street. Once they fought with teeth and claws, now they fight with wealth and power. And only one man can stop them... if he dares.

Also by Donna Ball

> **The Ladybug Farm series**
> *For every woman who ever had a dream... or a friend*
>
> **A Year on Ladybug Farm**
> **At Home on Ladybug Farm**
> **Love Letters from Ladybug Farm**
> **Christmas on Ladybug Farm**
> **Recipes from Ladybug Farm**
> **Vintage Ladybug Farm**

~

ABOUT THE AUTHOR….

Donna Ball is the author of over a hundred novels under several different pseudonyms in a variety of genres that include romance, mystery, suspense, paranormal, western adventure, historical and women's fiction. Recent popular series include the Ladybug Farm series by Berkley Books and the Raine Stockton Dog Mystery series. Donna is an avid dog lover and her dogs have won numerous titles for agility, obedience and canine musical freestyle. She lives in a restored Victorian Barn in the heart of the Blue Ridge mountains with a variety of four-footed companions. You can contact her at http://www.donnaball.net.

6936654R00204

Made in the USA
San Bernardino, CA
17 December 2013